MATT DICKINSON

North Face.

A special thank you to Sarah Darby
for the chapter heading illustrations.

Also by Matt Dickinson

Mortal Chaos

Black Ice

The Death Zone

The Everest Files

MATT DICKINSON

North Face.

North Face
Matt Dickinson

First published in 2016 by Vertebrate Publishing.

Vertebrate Publishing
Crescent House, 228 Psalter Lane, Sheffield, S11 8UT, UK
www.v-publishing.co.uk

A CIP catalogue record for this book is available from the British Library.

ISBN 978-1-910240-46-5 (Paperback)
ISBN 978-1-910240-47-2 (eBook)

10 9 8 7 6 5 4 3 2 1

Production by Vertebrate Publishing
www.v-publishing.co.uk

Vertebrate Publishing is committed to printing on paper from sustainable sources.

Printed and bound in Great Britain by
Clays Ltd, St Ives plc

For my son

Dani

CHAPTER 1

EVEREST BASE CAMP
TIBET

The bus wheezed and spluttered as it struggled up the pass. Steam began to spew out of the engine bay. I heard the driver crunch down the gears, grumbling as the machine lost power.

Finally, just as it seemed the vehicle would suffer a mechanical heart attack, the driver coaxed a few more revs out of the old wreck and we lurched up the last switchback turn, arriving at a flat section of road adorned with brightly coloured prayer flags and Buddhist cairns.

The engine shuddered with a metallic clanking noise as the driver turned it off.

'Good photo place!' our guide exclaimed.

We climbed out of the cab. None of us uttered a sound, not wanting to spoil the moment with meaningless words of wonder. The only noise was the fluttering of the little silk pennants rippling in the light wind.

I let my eyes drink in the view. Twenty-five miles from our viewpoint stood the most stunning mountain vista I had ever seen.

Everest.

This was the vision of the mountain that I had heard so much about. The view of the North Face seen from the high passes of the Tibetan plateau.

'We've got a word in English,' I told my travelling companion, Klaus. 'We call something like this "gobsmacking".'

'*Gobsmacking?*' Klaus repeated with relish, his thick German accent giving bizarre emphasis to the word.

I wished my Nepali friend Kami could have been with me at that moment. It was him that had inspired me to make this journey. He had once climbed to within a stone's throw of the summit. Everest was a part of him; he would have loved this view. I felt Kami's presence. Almost like he was standing there beside me.

At that moment I reached into the side pocket of my fleece. The pocket that held the tiny metal shrine bell,

Kami's most treasured possession. The brass seemed strangely warm to the touch, almost as if the proximity to Everest had fired up some unexpected power within it.

I shivered. I wasn't superstitious but I did sometimes wonder about this precious object which had been passed to my care.

A truck full of Chinese troops suddenly swept past at speed. The daydream was shattered.

A dozen ravens took flight, rising from nearby rocks, their wings beating black and hard against the thin air. The ground shuddered. Just the slightest tremor.

'What was that ... ?' Klaus laughed nervously.

△

The camp at the foot of the North Col was a bustling hub of human activity: hundreds of red, yellow and green tents were clustered on the glacial terrain, yaks arriving continuously, carrying the special blue equipment barrels that seem universal to every expedition.

'There must be a thousand people here!' Klaus exclaimed.

There was an incredible energy to the place, the air filled with a distinctive mix of scents: kerosene, perfumed glacier cream, the pungent smell of animal dung.

'I smell bacon,' I told Klaus. The tantalising aroma of

cooked breakfast was seeping from a nearby mess tent. 'Must be Brits around!'

Many of the teams had hoisted their national flags outside their camps. We took a walk; heard Russian voices laughing across the moraine. A team from Iran were newly arrived. Climbers from the Basque country of Spain were eating breakfast al fresco, sitting around a gas stove outside their mess tent.

Then, amongst the chaos, someone caught my eye. It was a girl, roughly my own age, leading three yaks into the camp.

At first I thought she was a Westerner, tricked by the fleece and trekking trousers she wore, but then, as she turned her head and we locked eyes for a moment, I saw her deeply tanned face and shoulder-length plaits of jet-black hair and realised it was a local Tibetan girl. I felt my breath catch.

She looked towards me, raised a camera and took a shot of me and Klaus. Then, with a cheeky smile, she turned back to her yaks.

'That's a pretty girl,' Klaus teased me. 'Love at first sight?'

I punched him lightly on the arm.

'Check out the mountain!' Klaus said suddenly.

Everest was illuminated by a burst of sunlight.

I took a series of photographs, pushing in ever closer with my telephoto lens to pick out details. I spotted the notches in the ridge that marked the famous 'first step', the notorious sections of almost vertical rock that cut into the climbing route. Further up was the even more impressive 'second step', the final cliff that guarded the summit ridge.

What would it be like to be up there? I wondered. In the Death Zone. Treading the wild margins between life and death. I felt a tinge of regret; the journey I was currently making was just a trek, a trip to Base Camp and no further. The permits and equipment to actually climb were far beyond my resources. For the moment.

'Seventy million years in the making and still rising by a few centimetres every year.' Klaus said.

'Let's go for a walk,' I said. 'Get some photos from a different angle.'

We crunched across the ice. A slight ache started to spread across the side of my chest. The thin air was causing me to breathe deeper than normal, stretching my chest muscles.

Fifteen minutes later we reached the viewpoint I had in mind.

And that was when the earthquake hit.

△

The earth gave a massive lurch and I was thrown to the ground, falling awkwardly. I hit the rocky floor of the glacier, the full weight of my body crashing on to my left wrist as I twisted instinctively to protect the camera.

Klaus stumbled but managed to stay upright.

'Was that what I think it was?' he said, his face pale.

Earthquake?

Stones clattered down the cliff face behind us. I sprang back to my feet, my heart thudding like crazy. Shouts rang out from the climbers down at the camp.

'Get away from the face!'

I looked up at the higher slopes which towered above us. At the ice fields, the vast quantity of wind-packed snow stacked a thousand metres above the camp.

'If that lot goes … '

The second tremor was more violent, the sound of it primeval. A dragon's roar. A grinding symphony of crushed rock that came from deep in the guts of the planet. Someone screamed. The ground shimmered. Dust plumed upwards.

A shark's fin serac of blue ice collapsed on the glacier about ten metres from us. Thousands of kilos of shattered ice went skittering across the ground.

'Look!' Klaus grabbed my arm and pointed at Everest.

I spun around. The entire face was alive with movement. Rock fall, avalanche, dust trails and ice flowing down the gullies and couloirs at incredible speed. For a split second I thought about the climbers in the high camps. They wouldn't stand a chance.

The ground shuddered again. A thunderous noise began.

Klaus screamed: 'Run!'

A cloud of ice and tumbling rock was racing down the sheer cliff behind us. We sprinted away from the face.

I think we managed about three strides.

△

The avalanche engulfed us. It felt like I'd been kicked in the back by a horse. I was blown off my feet, sent head over heels. Klaus smashed into me, our heads knocked together.

A fusillade of cracks and clunks came out of the dense cloud. Stone on stone. Stone on ice. Bullet-like impacts, half-seen objects flashing past in a blur of darkness. I kept my head down, skidding with my cheek pressed against gritty, frozen mud.

I snatched a look. Klaus had his head up. *Idiot!*

'Get down!'

A rock the size of a suitcase tumbled out of the void and smashed itself to smithereens on a boulder little more than an arm's length from our position. An even bigger missile went whirring overhead, disappearing into the white nightmare.

'We have to get away from the face! Come on!' Klaus yelled. He stood, moving quickly into the ice cloud.

I tried to stand. A frozen block cut through the avalanche, hitting me square in the ribs, smashing all the air out of my lungs.

'Ryan … ?' Klaus called back.

A dense thud came through the silver haze. A sharp exhalation of air. The sound of a human body hitting the ground. The voice was cut off.

I spat out pieces of gravel. Stars exploded across my vision. I drew in a huge breath, shivering as crystals of ice got sucked into my lungs. Ice fragments continued to zip out of nowhere. Smaller stones and pebbles.

I scrambled up, managed to get on to all fours, still winded from the blow.

A figure appeared by my side, the face slowly coming into focus. It was the Tibetan girl – the one who had been leading the yaks. She looked bruised and covered in dust but otherwise in one piece.

'Are you OK?' she said.

'Can't … breathe … '

'Come on!' She yanked me upright and got my arm over her shoulders.

An aftershock undulated through the ground. The earthquake wasn't done yet. A deep boom announced a further avalanche, somewhere far away on the other side of the valley.

'Where's my friend?' I gasped.

I looked for Klaus, my guts twisting with dread.

Footsteps. A Sherpa came stumbling out of the gloom. Blood was dripping from a deep cut on his forehead.

'This way! Quickly!' he shouted. He pointed urgently into the ice cloud then vanished as swiftly as he had appeared, tripping unsteadily away.

'Can you walk now?' the girl asked.

Air flowed into my lungs. I gasped with relief. My rib-cage flared with pain.

'I guess.'

Seconds ticked by. The avalanche cloud began to clear.

Gradually the destruction became visible. The scene reminded me of battlefield photographs from the First World War.

'Klaus?' I called.

There was no reply.

△

The camp had been trashed. Hundreds of tents wiped away. Everything had been torn to the ground or spirited skywards in the blast.

'The gods have spoken ... ' the girl said quietly.

Crumpled figures were lying prone, many with gruesome injuries. We saw a climber with a broken neck, his head almost severed from his body. Expedition medics were running to help their teammates, or rummaging amongst the wreckage of their tents for first aid kits. Distressed voices rang out across the glacier, calling for lost friends.

'Klaus!' I yelled again. No answer came.

I heard the sound of a camera shutter. A Western photographer was standing nearby, taking shots of the scene. I realised with a sick feeling that he was filming the bodies.

'Klaus!'

We walked forward for ten or fifteen paces, finding odd bits of kit scattered around. Much of it was buried beneath the ice blocks that had cascaded down the cliff. We smelled gas, found one of the propane cylinders spewing its contents into the air. I turned off the valve. The girl stepped over to a deep crevasse.

'Look!'

I went to join her, staring into the depths at an extraordinary confusion of smashed-up camp equipment. In the midst of it all a boot and section of lower leg could be seen sticking out. I felt acid rising in my throat.

Klaus's boot.

'It's my friend,' I said.

The boot twitched.

'Quickly!' the girl exclaimed.

She jumped down into the shallow end of the crevasse without a moment's hesitation. I gritted my teeth and slid down next to her.

'We need something to dig with,' she said. We found a squashed saucepan and a baking tray amongst the debris.

The boot moved again. Klaus was buried head down. Entombed. Held fast in the grip of the ice.

The Tibetan girl was quick and strong, scraping out quantities of the rock-hard ice with each swing of her arms. I did the same with the metal tray, slicing down into the debris and throwing it into the far end of the crevasse.

I was soon out of breath.

'He felt us!' she said.

Klaus's legs kicked. Half remembered facts from a documentary flashed into my mind: how long avalanche victims have got before they suffocate. Fifteen minutes? That was the figure that came to mind. But I wasn't sure.

His waist was now exposed.

Dig. Dig. The girl was incredible, working twice as fast as me.

'Pull now!' she said.

I paused to draw oxygen into my lungs. I was dizzy, feeling faint. My chest ached with the effort of sucking in that super-thin air. The Tibetan girl took one leg. I took the other.

'Go!' she said.

We pulled like crazy.

Nothing happened. He was stuck fast.

'Harder!' the girl hissed.

We tugged with all our might. Klaus's upper body slipped suddenly free from the ice. He drew in a massive breath, flopping on to his side like a landed fish. His lips were bright blue. His face was creased with pain and shock.

'What took you so long?' he gasped.

△

Klaus was evacuated by military helicopter one hour later. The bodies of two dead climbers were loaded in beside him. My German friend was one of the lucky ones.

'He's inhaled a lot of ice,' an expedition doctor told me as the helicopter flew off down the valley. 'His lungs could take a couple of weeks to recover.'

'He's tough,' the girl told me. 'I get the feeling he'll be fine.'

I nodded my agreement.

'You saved his life,' I told her. 'What's your name?'

'Tashi.'

'Ryan.'

We stood there awkwardly. I saw her turn and look up towards the mountain.

'What are you going to do now?' I asked.

A shadow fell across her face.

'I have to find out about my brother.'

'Your *brother*?' I looked around the devastated camp. 'Was he here when the earthquake hit?'

She bit her lip, continued staring up at the mountain. Then she spoke slowly.

'No. He was up there. At Camp 6. Helping an expedition.'

I thought back to the rock and ice avalanches that had swept the upper slopes of Everest. It was hard to imagine that anyone could have survived.

'Maybe we can find some information,' I suggested. 'Which team was he with?'

'They were from Switzerland.'

We stumbled around the glacier for a while, asking for

the whereabouts of the team. Finally we found a tent with a Swiss flag fluttering above it, one of the very few that hadn't been destroyed. There was no one inside so we waited at the table for a while. Half an hour later a Sherpa man came in, limping heavily with a bloodied bandage round his leg.

'I haven't got anything to tell you,' he told us sadly. 'All I know is your brother was up there with one other climber.'

The Sherpa directed us to a large green tent stationed in the centre of the glacier. The buzz of urgent conversation came from inside.

'The Base Camp commander is in there,' he said. 'Maybe he can tell you more.'

We walked across the ice and pushed our way into the mess tent. The space was crammed with climbers all trying to talk at once. A radio set was squawking at high volume. In the middle of the mayhem a bad-tempered-looking Chinese military officer was fielding questions from the assembled expeditioners.

'You will get news when we have it!' he repeated over and over again. 'Now please leave the tent!'

The climbers showed no signs of leaving, but redoubled their efforts to get the man's attention.

I followed Tashi as she pushed her way through the crowd with grim determination. To my surprise the Base Camp commander seemed to recognise her, his face set instantly into a hostile stare.

'What do you want?' he asked.

'My brother Karma is at Camp 6,' she said. 'Do you have any information about him?'

'Your brother can't be on the mountain,' the commander said coldly. 'He hasn't got a permit.'

'He is there,' Tashi replied emphatically. 'Permit or not.'

The commander shook his head.

'Everyone at Camp 6 is dead,' he said firmly. 'You should forget about your brother.'

He stared at her with a strangely unsettling look and I saw Tashi wince.

'Now let me get on with my job!' he snapped.

We left the tent and stood in the freezing air for a few moments.

'He's under pressure,' I said finally. 'He probably didn't mean to be rude ... '

Tashi didn't say anything but it was clear from her frown she didn't agree with what I'd said. I felt a bit stupid; why was I trying to make excuses for that guy? He obviously hated Tashi for some reason.

'I don't believe him,' she said stubbornly. 'I'm sure Karma is still alive.'

The ground shivered with an aftershock. Pebbles tumbled down a nearby slope.

I suddenly thought back to the first time I had seen her.

'Where are your animals?' I asked.

Tashi's face clouded. She pointed to the other side of the camp.

'This way,' she said uncertainly. 'They were tethered by those rocks.'

We walked for a few minutes, through further scenes of devastation. Climbers were working to rebuild their tents. Helicopters were still flying in to the makeshift landing pad to pick up the wounded.

Suddenly Tashi stopped, a new expression of horror passing across her face. We were looking at a messed-up patch of ground. Avalanche debris had reached even this remote spot. There were boulders and piles of ice everywhere.

'They were here,' Tashi said quietly. 'I thought they would have been safe … '

We stepped towards the small river that was cut in the glacier surface.

'Oh no!' Tashi ran forward. As I stepped beside her I saw three dark shapes entwined in a macabre embrace at the far end of the stream where it plunged into a hole in the glacier surface. Three yaks. Drowned. Swept into the river by the avalanche.

Tashi put a hand to her mouth. She stifled a sob.

I stood there, unsure what I could possibly do to help. I felt terrible for her. Her brother missing on Everest. All three of her yaks killed.

At that moment a bitter wind sprang up. The air felt bruised and heavy, like a storm was on the way. We retrieved the bag containing Tashi's belongings from the river. Everything was soaked. Even her sleeping bag and tent were sopping wet.

'What are you going to do?' I asked her.

'I don't know,' she said. Her worried eyes flashed with determination. 'But I won't leave this place while my brother is in danger.'

I felt an overwhelming sense of sorrow for her. A need to help.

'We can make a shelter,' I said. 'But we'd better move fast.'

△

We began to scour the area, looking for canvas and tent poles. Within fifteen minutes we had collected a couple of fly-sheets and a heavy panel of Dacron from the piles of debris.

'A stove!' Tashi found a small cooker which looked like it might work.

Using lightweight para cord, we lashed the various bits of flysheet and canvas over four tent poles, creating a ramshackle shelter. There was no groundsheet, but a couple of strategically placed foam mats would protect us from the frozen glacier surface. Tashi fired up the little stove and put a pan of ice on to melt. We held our hands towards the flame, savouring the welcome wave of warmth coming off it.

'When was the last time you ate?' I asked her.

She shrugged.

'I had some rice last night.'

I found a Mars bar in my pack, split it in two and shared it with her. The taste was wonderfully sweet, a comforting burst of sugar.

'You're shivering,' she said.

Luckily I still had my sleeping bag and we soon found Klaus's bag inside his abandoned pack. We zipped them together to form one giant sleeping sack for the two of us, glad of the shared body warmth against the cold.

'What are your plans now your friend has gone?' Tashi asked. 'Will you still try to climb?'

'Climb Everest?' I had to smile at the idea. 'In my dreams! I'm just here on a trek. Travelling and taking photographs.'

I brought Tashi up to speed on the gap-year journey I was making, telling her also about the magical time I had recently had in Nepal, working for a medical charity.

'I should have been home by now,' I continued. 'Working on my mum and dad's farm before going to university. But I extended my trip, had to get a close-up look at Everest.'

'Obsession,' Tashi said flatly. 'Like my brother.'

'Definitely,' I agreed. 'Plus there is something else.'

I pulled the shrine bell from my fleece pocket and handed it to Tashi.

'My Nepali friend Kami took this with him when he climbed Everest,' I told her. 'He wanted to put it on the summit but never quite made it.'

Tashi turned the pretty little bell in her hands.

'These items are sacred,' she said. 'Powerful. The prayers of generations locked inside them.'

'My friend wants me to get it to Everest summit one day,' I told her, feeling slightly foolish. 'Finish the quest.'

'If the gods allow, anything is possible,' Tashi replied.

She handed the shrine bell back.

I thought about Tashi's brother, caught up there on the highest slopes of Everest. The chances of him still being alive seemed increasingly small.

'How old is Karma?' I asked her.

'Fifteen.'

I stared at her in surprise. I had imagined he would be much older.

'Isn't he a bit young to be climbing Everest?'

'Yes,' Tashi agreed. I could see she was close to tears.

She pulled a battered postcard from her pocket. I saw that it was a portrait of the Dalai Lama, the spiritual leader of the Tibetan people. I knew that he had been exiled from Tibet for most of his life, hounded out of the country after the Chinese invaded.

Tashi mumbled a prayer as she viewed the picture.

'So how come your brother's up there?'

'It's a long story,' she said.

I noticed a dark stain across the photograph. I took it from her and looked at it closely.

'That looks like blood,' I said. 'What happened?'

Tashi sighed, drew out a long, deep breath.

Then she began to talk.

CHAPTER 2

It was late spring on the plateau of Tibet. Streams were alive with meltwater. Butterflies were making their first tentative forays into the air, miraculously alive after being cocooned through the long Himalayan winter, the deepest and coldest on earth.

An eagle circled in an electric blue sky. A sky so dark it looked like a splash of deep space had accidentally been mixed in.

Tashi and her family had just arrived at the windswept grassy plain where the summer festival would be held. Snow-capped mountains glimmered in the distance. Everest was among them, mysterious behind a translucent veil of wispy cloud. Tashi felt a tingle of excitement run up her spine. Hundreds of nomadic families were arriving. The games were set to begin.

'This will be your year,' her father told her earnestly as they looked out across the lively scene. 'The white scarf will be yours.'

Tashi let her imagination soar, wondering if she could win the horse race that she had entered for the following day. It would take all her skill in the saddle, and plenty of courage as well. She had seen the risks such races involved, the broken legs and arms that came with a fall beneath thundering hooves. Occasionally there were fatalities but with luck she would snatch the white scarf from the ground; be the first girl ever to win the trophy.

Tashi and her father walked through the festival site, enjoying the bustle as the traders set up their stalls. Tantalising aromas filled the air; spicy *momo* dumplings frying in bubbling oil, sweet rice puddings known as *dresil*, filled with dried cherries, pecans and pine nuts.

A green Chinese army truck pulled up nearby.

'Lots of soldiers this year,' her father commented grimly.

A line of stern-faced young troops marched past. Tashi heard the crackle of walkie-talkies, the language alien to her. Tibet had been an autonomous region of China for two generations now but relations were strained and the people of this remote plateau still yearned for independence.

'Come to enjoy the show?' Tashi asked with a wry smile.

'Maybe.'

Families from all over the plateau were already pitching their tents. A thousand Tibetan nomads would arrive in the next twenty-four hours, each dressed in their finest clothes. Then the festivities would start: archery competitions to decide the finest shot; wrestling for trophies; and the horse races in which Tashi excelled.

It was a celebration of life in Tibet. A celebration of what it meant to be a nomad on the highest plateau on earth.

'Don't you think the atmosphere is a bit tense?' her father said.

Tashi looked about: it was true that there were large groups of nomad youths hanging around looking restless, eyes darting every so often towards the troops. In the distance Tashi saw a convoy of army trucks moving along a dusty highway. They slowed, turning towards the festival field.

'Where's Karma?' she asked, suddenly feeling her heartbeat quicken.

Tashi realised she hadn't seen her younger brother all day.

△

Tashi split from her father and found some friends.

'Have you seen Karma?'

They shook their heads.

A truck pulled up right next to them, a contingent of soldiers climbing out, wide-eyed young men, looking as out of place as if they had been dumped on the far side of the moon.

'This means trouble,' one of Tashi's friends muttered.

Tashi felt she was probably right.

The arrival of military personnel at the festival was no surprise to the young Tibetans. The previous two years had seen a huge increase in the amount of Chinese troops in almost every part of Tibet. Every town, every village, every monastery had soldiers attached, watching the local population with obsessive zeal, intent on sniffing out rebellion or dissent even if it was entirely imaginary.

The troops were young and ambitious, keen to prove themselves to their superiors. Snooping on the local populace was encouraged, spying almost endemic. Promotion could follow the arrest or detention of a local Tibetan. Tashi and her friends mostly kept their distance.

Suddenly Tashi saw her brother. He was wrestling two other lads on a patch of wasteland. One of them was a good head taller than Karma but Tashi's younger brother was fast and strong for his age.

'Karma!' she shouted. Her brother made a lightning move, picked up the bigger boy as if he was a sack of potatoes.

'Hey!' she called, louder. Tashi couldn't help smiling as the fight became critical.

Karma body-slammed his opponent into the dirt, a thick plume of dust rising up in a cloud. His opponent groaned, conceding defeat with a wave of his hand. Karma walked up to his sister, brushing dust off his clothes as he came.

'Want to try your luck?' he asked her. 'Best of three falls?'

'No thanks,' Tashi replied with a big grin. 'I wouldn't want to embarrass you in front of your friends.'

At that moment three of the soldiers marched past. Karma winked at his buddies and started to follow them.

'Karma!' Tashi hissed. She snatched at his arm but he shrugged her off with a laugh.

He fell in at the back of the stern-faced young conscripts, goose-stepping comically behind them to the delight of his buddies.

'You!'

The voice bellowed from a nearby jeep. An officer stepped out, dressed in a crisp uniform, three golden stars glinting in the sun.

Karma froze in his tracks, turning abruptly.

'Captain Chen,' one of Tashi's friends muttered. 'I know him, he's always looking for trouble.'

Tashi groaned beneath her breath. Typical Karma, she thought, always in the wrong place at the wrong time.

Karma stood there, staring at his feet as the military man strode up.

'You think it's a good idea to disrespect my soldiers?' he barked.

'It was just a joke, sir,' Karma replied.

'A joke? Those are representatives of the People's Army, here for the protection of us all, guarding the border zone day and night. There are enemies out there. Counter revolutionaries. You think that's a *joke*?'

'No sir.'

'Let me see what you have in your pockets,' Chen ordered.

Karma's eyes flitted to Tashi, his cockiness completely gone.

'Come on boy, quickly!'

Karma reached into his trouser pockets, bringing out some coins and a twist of twine.

'Now that one … '

Karma brought out a small silver locket.

'Not carrying drugs I hope?' He opened the tiny silver box.

'No sir. Just some lucky beads.'

The army man tossed the small jade beads in his hand. Then he placed them none too carefully back into the silver box and snapped it shut.

'How about your jacket?' the officer said. 'What have you got in there?'

Karma did not move.

The officer reached out and searched Karma's top pockets, grunting as he found a small plastic wallet. Tashi held her breath. The man opened the wallet and found a photograph inside.

Karma went white in the face. Chen plucked the photograph from the wallet and held it right in front of Karma's nose.

'Who is this?' he said quietly.

Tashi felt her heart beating hard against her ribs.

'Well?'

'It's the Dalai Lama, sir … '

'You know it is illegal to own a photograph of this so-called holy man?'

Karma nodded miserably.

'So? What are you doing with it?'

'I was given it, sir. I forgot it was there.'

'You will be punished for this,' Chen said. 'Where do you stay?'

'With my f ... f ... family,' Karma stammered. He looked across to Tashi and the officer spun round to follow his eyeline.

'Who are you?'

'I'm his sister.'

'Come here!' the officer ordered. Tashi walked over.

'Do you also break the law with images of this criminal?'

Tashi shook her head. 'No, sir.'

Chen thought for a few moments. His eyes bored into Karma with terrifying intensity.

'Maybe I should investigate further,' he said.

The soldier ordered the brother and sister to take him to the family tent.

△

Karma led the way across the festival site to the place where the family were camped. The officer picked up two young soldiers on the way. Tashi wanted to yell a warning to her parents but she knew it would only make things worse.

A few of the other nomads were watching from near-by. Their mouths fell open when they saw Chen and his guards marching towards them.

In years gone by the military would never have bothered

them at the festival. Just left them in peace. Clearly those days were over.

'This is our place,' Karma told him nervously.

The officer pulled aside the felt covering that served as a door and stepped in without announcing himself. Tashi and Karma followed, seeing their parents turn in astonishment as they saw the soldiers standing there. It was extremely discourteous for any visitor to enter without uttering a friendly greeting from outside.

'Karma? What's happened?' Tashi's father scrambled up from the blankets where he had been resting.

Chen held up the portrait of the Dalai Lama.

'Your son had this in his pocket,' he told them. 'Do you have anything to say?'

Karma hung his head. The only sound in the tent was the bubbling of the rice pot. Tashi felt her spine chilling.

'Perhaps the whole family needs to be investigated,' Chen proposed. 'Maybe you are all collaborators of this criminal?'

Tashi's father stepped forward, raising his hands in a conciliatory gesture.

'I'm sure this is all an unfortunate misunderstanding,' he said. 'The boy must have been given the portrait and forgotten to destroy it.'

'On the contrary,' the officer countered. 'The portrait was obviously a treasured possession. I fear your son has been brainwashed by counter revolutionaries.'

Tashi and her mother exchanged a horrified look. The soldier was trying to make it seem like Karma was some sort of terrorist. Just for carrying a picture of the Dalai Lama. It was so unjust it made Tashi want to weep.

The man looked around the tent then crossed to the sleeping area. He opened up some storage trunks and poked around amongst the clothes they contained.

'Perhaps you are members of a cell,' he snapped. 'Maybe in contact with the criminal himself in his Indian headquarters?'

Then he found the family strongbox.

'Open it,' he ordered.

'Please … no,' Tashi protested. 'Those things are private …'

Chen nodded at one of the guards. Tashi was pushed roughly to one side.

'Break the lock,' Chen commanded.

The soldier smashed the small padlock with the butt of his gun. It yielded on the third blow, and he flipped open the lid of the trunk. Chen began to rummage through the contents of the trunk, throwing family photographs and small religious figurines on to the blankets.

'You have no right ... ' Tashi's mother said.

A small porcelain Buddha broke in two as it tumbled to the floor. The military man poked among the possessions for a while then seemed to bore of it. He walked up to Karma, gripping the young boy's chin hard in his right hand.

'I never forget a face,' he said.

Then he walked out of the tent.

△

The long winter months crawled by. Hard for the yaks. Harder still for the family. The incident at the festival was never spoken about but it haunted them all the same; the family had left that very same night, Tashi abandoning her hopes to compete in the races.

Now it was time to pack up the family possessions. Winter was over and the trek to the summer grazing grounds was about to begin.

'Go and find Karma will you?' Tashi's mother asked.

Her younger brother had made himself scarce as usual when hard work was to be done.

Tashi found him by the lake, messing about on a battered old motorbike belonging to some friends.

'Come on!' she goaded him. 'Mother will go nuts if you don't come and help.'

A mixture of threats and persuasion dragged Karma back to the family tent and the process of loading up the yaks began.

Cooking utensils and fodder, blankets and fence posts, coils of rope, blocks of salt, the hundreds of simple items that make up the world of a nomadic family. A family that considers the plateau their spiritual home. A family that lives beneath the stars and adapts with the ever-changing seasons so that it is perfectly in tune with the land.

'One day I'm going to be rich,' Karma said. 'Buy a motorbike of my own and go round the world.'

Karma's crazy comments made Tashi laugh.

'You can't even afford a *bicycle*,' she teased. 'Get real.'

They dismantled the family tent, unpicking the threads that held the felt panels together. Tashi tied the bundles tight with cord, helped by her brother.

'Look what I bought,' Karma said. 'You see how they can't stop me?'

He showed Tashi a new photograph of the Dalai Lama that he kept in his top pocket. Tashi said nothing. Silently she applauded his bravado.

The yaks took their loads with bad-tempered grunts.

The winter had been long and hard for them and they were out of sorts with the world. Dried hay had kept them alive but Tashi knew they craved the lush grass of the summer grazing lands. With every year of her life she had seen the animals' mood improve dramatically once they got to the valley.

'Ya!' Tashi's mother gave the nearest yak a warning stroke of her stick.

The twenty yaks ambled up the trail, gradually forming a long wavering line. Tashi stepped alongside them, feeling a glow of pleasure as she looked forward to the trek.

'Feels good to be on the move, doesn't it?' her father said.

Tashi nodded.

The trek would take one week, passing through the mountains on narrow shepherds' trails. Tashi found it refreshing to walk for hours each day, the chores of winter seeming like a distant dream as they passed through high mountain glades, carpeted with a profusion of spring flowers. Occasionally they found isolated tents, a lonely man or two tending a huge flock of sheep. Invariably they would be invited in for butter tea, swapping news from the plateau as bread and cheese was shared.

'Have you heard the rumours?' one shepherd asked them gravely. 'Soldiers are closing off the land.'

‘There are stories,’ Tashi’s father replied cautiously. ‘But we haven’t seen any troops for a while.’

‘Better to keep it that way,’ the man said.

They continued, and, with each passing day, Tashi found herself lighter of spirit.

As they climbed up the final sloping path, Tashi picked up her pace. The long trek was almost over and the view from the top of the ridge was something that she relished. For years she had always been the first one of the family to reach that place.

She remembered it as a gorgeous view; a wide and fertile valley locked between two snow-capped mountain slopes. From that lofty vantage point, the entire grazing area was laid out, thick pastures of lush grass stretching for kilometres. Several streams tumbled off the higher peaks. It was an idyllic place to pass the summer. An opportunity for the yaks to build up fat. A chance for the family to enjoy their time together.

Tashi climbed, her heart filled with expectation. As she got closer to the ridge, Tashi heard the rumble of engines. Closer still she could see clouds of red dust filling the air. She slowed, frowning as she tried to work out what was going on.

She reached the top. Then stopped dead.

A road was being constructed. Just over the ridgeline. Bulldozers and earth movers were scraping into the bedrock of the valley wall. A line of heavy trucks was queuing to drop tarmac on to the newly graded surface. Fifty or sixty Tibetan workers were raking the hot tarmac into place. A dozen Chinese supervisors watched them impassively, clipboards clutched in their hands. The noise was horrendous. Rock was splitting and cracking. Pneumatic drills rattled a metallic serenade into the air. The road stretched away into the far distance. As far as the eye could see.

Tashi felt her stomach tighten as her brother Karma came up next to her.

'What's going on?' he said. 'Have we come to the wrong place?'

'No. It's the right place,' Tashi said sadly.

Karma put his hands to his ears.

'What are they doing?' he shouted.

△

Their father joined them, all the colour draining from his face as he saw the mess the road makers had created.

At that moment Tashi spotted a military man. He was talking excitedly into a radio set and gesturing towards them.

'I think he's talking about us,' Tashi said nervously.

The moment the soldier ended his radio call the family heard a roar of different engines. A couple of military trucks came speeding round the bend in the road.

'Now we've got trouble,' Tashi's father muttered.

The army vehicles came to a halt on the other side of the road, the soldiers inside them jumping out with their guns at the ready. Her father put a reassuring hand on Tashi's shoulder.

'I'm sure they are just lost,' he told her.

Tashi felt dozens of staring eyes locked on to her. She wasn't sure she liked the expression on the faces of the young soldiers.

'They're looking at us like we've done something wrong,' she said.

'Just ignore them,' her father replied, 'I'll go and talk with the commander.'

'I'll come with you,' Tashi offered.

'No,' he told her hastily. 'You stay with Karma and Mother. Better I deal with them alone.'

Tashi and Karma turned around and started off back down the track. As they went their father called after them:

'Don't let your mother come up here. I don't want her to see this.'

They intercepted their mother halfway up the hill.

'The Chinese are in our valley?' she raged. 'Let me go up there and see about that!'

She made to race up the slope but Tashi and her brother held her back. Somehow they managed to stop her.

They found a small glade where the yaks could rest, hobbling the creatures to wait for their father to return. They rigged up the tent. Their mother brewed a kettle for tea but they found they had little appetite to drink or eat.

'Until now we have been lucky,' Tashi heard her mother say. 'There had to be a day when the Chinese would stand in our way.'

One hour passed. Then another. Tashi found her imagination running wild. Where was her father?

'What's happening up there?' Tashi's mother wailed. 'How long does it take to tell them to leave?'

'Perhaps he had to go to see a supervisor,' Tashi reassured her. 'We must stay calm.'

Finally they heard the noise of the tent fabric being pulled back. Tashi's father's face was grey. A nervous tic was pulling at the muscles of his cheek, something Tashi had never seen before.

'The soldier says the valley is closed,' he said grimly. 'The land is to become a national park, no people are allowed.'

There was a long silence as the family digested this unappetising revelation.

'You mean, we can't go into the valley today?' Tashi asked. Her young mind had failed to understand the enormity of the news.

Her father sighed.

'It means we can't go in forever,' he said. 'It's over.'

Tashi's mother stepped forward. She clutched her husband's hand.

'There must be some mistake,' she said. 'Our families have always used this land.'

'I told them that,' Tashi's father said. 'They say it makes no difference.'

'What are they going to do with this "national park"?' Tashi's mother asked. 'What's the point of it?'

Her father took a long sip of tea.

'They said the land is destroyed by animals grazing,' he said. 'They want to preserve it.'

'Preserve it?' Karma spat. 'It's not even their land in the first place.'

'They asked me for paperwork. Documents to prove that we had a right to graze the land. Of course I had nothing.'

'You had nothing because such papers don't exist!' Tashi's mother stabbed at her thigh with her finger as she spoke each word. 'We have the right to graze this land in summer because of the hundreds of years our families have been here! It has always been this way.'

'They don't care about that,' Karma said. 'They want to mess us up, that's all.'

'They can't stop us taking our animals in there!' Tashi said angrily. 'We will fight them if they try!'

Karma leapt up: 'Yes! That's the answer!'

'Fight them?' Tashi's father laughed bitterly.

He pulled back the tent wall so they could see up the slope.

'You see that?' he said. 'That's what you'll be battling against.'

Tashi looked out, seeing that the military vehicles were now lined up on the ridgeline, overlooking their campsite. Each one was packed full of armed troops, staring down on them with hostile expressions.

'Oh,' she whispered. 'I see.'

△

'Where will we go?' Karma asked angrily. 'How can we feed the yaks when we can't give them good grazing?'

'There are other places,' his father replied. 'Maybe we will get lucky.'

'They need high ground,' Tashi reminded him. 'The yaks will get sick if we have to go beneath three thousand metres. We should insist on staying.'

'We cannot insist on anything. There's nothing we can do.'

Tashi stared at her father. She felt a hot flush of anger in her cheeks. Why was he giving in so easily?

'You want to let them win?'

'It's not a question of winning or losing,' he replied. 'You cannot "win" against the authorities. Not by force, at least. We have to take the example of the Dalai Lama, make prayer our focus.'

The family stayed in that spot for the night, watched over non-stop by a contingent of troops. At daybreak they packed up the tent and trekked for a few hours with their yaks to a small valley much further down which might offer a few weeks of grazing.

To their surprise, even though the place was too low for the yaks to be truly healthy, there were five or six other families already there, each with their herds of livestock.

'This land will be exhausted in no time at all,' Tashi's father said as they looked at the scene.

The other families welcomed them with genuine warmth, but their stories were bleak. All of them had been turned off their ancestral grazing lands, displaced by Chinese officials for a variety of reasons, each more distressing than the last.

'They've built a dam across the end of our summer lands,' one nomad raged bitterly. 'By this time next year the whole area will be drowned beneath a lake.'

'There's a mine being constructed on ours,' another herder complained. 'A hundred trucks every hour running down a new road. So much dust the grass has turned white.'

Tashi's father's prediction proved correct. The small valley could not sustain so many horses, yaks, sheep and goats, the grass cropped right down as the animals ate their fill. By midsummer the small patch of grazing was dried out and worthless, not a lush blade of grass in sight.

The yaks began to sicken as parasites attacked. They were so finely adapted to the thin air above three thousand metres that this lower place made them ill. The families remained, hoping that summer rains might replenish the grass.

One day a small convoy of vehicles pulled up next to the family camp.

'Visitors,' Tashi's father said ominously.

Tashi felt her heart lurch in her chest. One of the vehicles was full of soldiers.

The family watched as workmen unloaded sections of steel fence from the back of a truck. They got to work, building a small temporary compound in less than an hour.

Later a Toyota jeep arrived, dropping off three men in white laboratory coats.

'What's going on?' Karma asked.

'I have no idea,' their father replied. 'But it doesn't look good.'

Boxes were taken from the Toyota and a table was erected. Medical instruments and glass containers were laid out on the surface. One of the men in white laboratory coats approached Tashi's father. Three soldiers walked behind him.

'We need to test your animals for disease,' he said.

No attempt at a greeting. No friendly hello. Just a raw statement.

'Disease?' Tashi's father said. 'What are you talking about? There's nothing wrong with them.'

'We will be the judge of that,' the man said. 'Bring them to us.'

Karma had been holding his tongue. Now he flared up.

'What if we don't want to?'

'The soldiers are here,' the man said. 'They can deal with you if necessary.' The military men scowled at Karma.

They looked like there was nothing they'd like more than to give him a good beating.

'It's just some basic medical tests,' the man continued soothingly. 'Nothing to be worried about so long as your herd is healthy.'

The yaks were taken into the metal compound one by one. The family could see that a number of procedures were carried out on each animal but when they tried to get closer the soldiers warned them away.

Finally the animals were released and the temporary compound was dismantled and loaded back on to the truck.

'Aren't you going to tell us something?' Tashi asked the men.

The scientists said nothing, just climbed into their vehicle and drove away.

△

A week went past. The family was on edge. Tashi and Karma spent a lot of time away from the camp, cutting grass with a scythe, then carrying it back to the herd in wicker baskets. Tashi would pile the cuttings right over her head. She had a special technique to tie it in a teetering tower on her back.

'You look like a mobile haystack!' Karma laughed.

The foraging expeditions became longer and longer. The family's herd had worked its way through all the lush grass within the radius of a one-hour walk. Her parents began to help with the grass collection, even though it meant leaving the camp vulnerable to an opportunistic thief or animal rustler.

'This place is a disaster,' her mother kept saying over and over. 'We will lose our herd this winter if we're not careful.'

The herd was not putting on enough weight. The animals were restless, tetchy with each other and their human guardians.

'They know they're being cheated out of their normal pasture,' Tashi said one night. 'They're not happy.'

Then, at dawn one morning, the ministry Toyota came back. The familiar truck full of soldiers followed it. Tashi was the first to spot them. She shook her family awake.

'Get up!' she told them urgently. Even Karma was quick to rise from his bed.

One of the men in the white lab coats got out and approached them with an attaché case in his hand. He walked into the tent and brought out some papers.

'Your herd is contaminated,' he said. 'We have an order to destroy it.'

A deep silence followed. Tashi was aware that even the yaks seemed to have become quiet, the normal lowing and grunting of early morning had mysteriously stopped.

'Contaminated?' Tashi's father said slowly. 'What on earth are you talking about?'

The man thrust some papers under Tashi's father's nose.

'Infested with parasites,' he snapped. 'Riddled with contagious diseases.'

He pointed at a long row of Chinese characters.

'Look at this list,' he said. 'Your herd must be destroyed immediately.'

CHAPTER 3

Tashi took the paper and read it out loud.

'Anthrax, ticks, salmonella, worms, tuberculosis … ' her voice tailed off as a lump grew in her throat.

'That's rubbish,' Karma said sharply. He pointed to the yaks. 'Look at them! They're not so bad!'

'They can spread diseases,' the man continued. 'We're going to destroy them before it's too late.'

'The things on your list are present in every animal,' Tashi's father explained patiently. 'I agree our herd is not in the best of condition but … '

'We had to bring the yaks down too low,' Karma cried out. 'Because our normal grazing grounds were blocked.'

The official riffled impatiently through the papers.

He found a page marked with a huge black stamp and showed it to them with a flourish.

'This is the official seal from Beijing,' he said grandly. 'Your herd will be destroyed in the next twenty-four hours and that is the end of it.'

'This is our livelihood,' Tashi's mother spat. 'You might as well put a gun to our heads and shoot us. It would have the same effect as taking away our yaks.'

'You will get compensation,' the man said. 'I will bring more forms to fill in soon.'

He replaced the papers in his attaché case and snapped it shut.

'I suggest you take your tent and go away from this place,' he said.

Then, with the soldiers in tow, he marched out.

Tashi's mother let out a cry of sheer desperation; over by the compound they could see two of the ministry men preparing huge syringes. With a sickening feeling in her guts Tashi realised they were preparing to put the animals to sleep right away.

'Follow me!' Karma yelled. He ran forward, overtaking the soldiers and the man from the ministry.

Tashi raced after her brother, the two of them holding hands and blocking the entrance to the enclosure where their animals were held.

'Please,' Tashi begged. 'You can't do this ... '

The parents ran to their children's side. The whole family linked arms, forming a fragile human barricade.

'Get them out of the way!' the officer commanded.

Half a dozen soldiers raced forward, their batons drawn. Two of them struck out at Karma, beating him on the shoulders and arms, sending him sprawling to the ground. The others attacked Tashi's father, pushing Tashi and her mother aside and throwing him backwards into a ditch filled with stagnant water and animal waste.

Tashi reached down to help him back out. He emerged spluttering and gasping for breath, his face rigid with shock. Karma groaned as he rolled in the dust. He got a couple more forceful blows to his arms and legs.

Suddenly one of the soldiers called out.

'Sir! Look!'

The officer frowned, looking round with a grunt of annoyance. Tashi turned, gasping out loud when she saw the crowd that had gathered: fifty or sixty nomads, all with anger written across their faces. The men were carrying staves.

Word of the family's problem had spread like wildfire through the valley.

△

'What are you doing?' the officer boldly addressed the crowd. The nomads just stood there, unsure, but united in their sense of outrage.

'Let the family alone!' came a voice. 'Leave their animals in peace.'

'They've done nothing wrong,' said another.

The officer talked urgently into his walkie-talkie.

A convoy of lumbering army trucks barged into the valley. Brakes squealed. Troops jumped from the tailgates, riot shields at the ready. Tashi saw a familiar figure among them: Captain Chen, a megaphone in hand.

'Disperse!' he shouted.

The nomads pushed back against the troops. Suddenly a rock came spinning through the air. It clattered against the helmet of a young soldier. Another stone hit Tashi on the shoulder.

Two sharp explosions cut through the cries of the protestors. Olive green metal canisters came skittering across the grass, right into the thick of the crowd. Dense white smoke plumed up in a hissing cloud. Tashi felt her throat tighten as a wave of gas was sucked into her lungs. Her eyes watered. She kicked one of the canisters away.

The troops began to lash out. The cries of anger from

the crowd grew louder. Fists were flying. Chen waded into the fray, taking out his baton and striking Tashi's father a fearsome blow right across the back.

Karma let out a cry of rage, leaping forward and twisting the baton out of the captain's hands. The stick whirled at lightning speed as Karma attacked. Chen staggered back, stunned. Then he blew furiously on his whistle, pointing directly at Karma.

'Arrest him!' he screamed.

A group of soldiers ran towards Karma, pushing back against the crowd as the nomads surged forward. Batons rained down in a haze of furious blows. Karma fell, blood gushing from a wound on his forehead.

Tashi crouched over her brother, trying to protect him from being crushed as dozens of Tibetans stampeded over them in a wave of thundering boots and flying bare feet. The megaphone continued to wail.

'Disperse!' Chen repeated. 'Disperse or we shoot.'

Tashi cried out as a sharp stripe of pain blazed across her legs.

'Leave him!' The soldier screamed.

Tashi felt strong hands pulling her away from Karma. She held on for dear life, her fingers quickly bent back almost to breaking point.

'It was self-defence,' Tashi shouted, 'Leave him!'

Karma shook himself as he regained consciousness. Tashi felt herself pulled roughly backwards. Her grip loosened. Her brother stood, pushing against the soldiers then turning to run. The megaphone blared again, Chen's voice sharper, more aggressive:

'Drop your weapons *now*!'

Tashi saw one of Karma's friends race in on his motorbike.

'Over here!' the friend called. Karma ran across and sprang on to the back.

The troops moved rapidly, trying to block the protestors as they regrouped. Tashi saw the motorbike weaving through the crowd.

'Go!' she muttered under her breath. 'Don't stop!'

Karma and his friend ripped away from the riot, heading up the dirt track at breakneck speed. The commander yelled again. A water cannon opened up, spraying a powerful jet at the Tibetans. Tashi got hit by the blast and was bowled off her feet. Visceral fear overwhelmed her for a few seconds as she struggled to breathe.

'Arrest them!' Chen ordered.

Tashi and her family were handcuffed and led to a military truck with twenty or more of the protestors.

'Where did Karma go?' Tashi's mother asked tearfully.

'Did he get away?'

Tashi pointed to a spot high on the mountainside where a tiny dot could just be seen. Karma and his friend were safely distant, looking down on the valley.

Half an hour later, with the family tent and all their other possessions thrown roughly into the back of the truck, they were driven away. Tashi took one last look at the yaks she had cared for all her life – the creatures she had loved and nurtured. She knew she would never see those animals again.

△

Tashi stared up at the black felt of the tent, listening to the restless creaking of the wooden poles as the flexing wind raced through, the occasional outburst of vicious barking from a nearby dog. The snorts and grunts of the yaks were missing. The chemistry of the night felt barren and wrong.

They were camping in a police compound, along with a bunch of other families who had been arrested after the protest. Her father was snoring lightly on the pile of blankets. From the corner of the tent came the sound of her mother weeping. Tashi got up and consoled her, stroking the side of her mother's head for a while until she fell into a restless sleep.

Then she heard a new noise, the stealthy sound of

footsteps padding towards the tent. Somehow she sensed it was Karma even before his dark shape slipped under the tent wall and came to her.

'You OK?' Tashi shuddered as she saw Karma's bruised and swollen face.

'More or less,' he tried a lopsided grin. Tashi felt a warm glow of love for her brother. It was amazing he could still smile after all that had happened in the last twenty-four hours.

'You're taking a massive risk sneaking in here,' she said.

Karma shrugged.

'Take more than a concrete wall to stop me!' he said.

'You're going to go away aren't you?' Tashi whispered.

Karma nodded sadly.

'Chen won't forget what I did,' he said. 'I fought back against him.'

'Sure. But he was beating Father. Beating an old man. You were right to resist.'

'It doesn't matter. They'll still send me to prison for sure.'

Tashi grimaced. She couldn't imagine her free-spirited brother being imprisoned. It would destroy him.

'Maybe you should escape with me?' he said.

Tashi had thought about it and already knew her answer.

'I can't leave Mother and Father,' she said. 'They need me.'

'I feel bad,' he said slowly. 'The authorities are going to make your life hell because of me.'

'How much worse can it be?' Tashi said. 'They've already destroyed our herd.'

Tashi pulled out her coat. There, in a secret pocket, she had some money saved.

'Take this,' she whispered.

Karma made to protest but Tashi pressed the small stack of notes into his hand.

'You're going to need it,' she said.

Karma nodded and tucked the notes away.

'Where will you go?' Tashi asked. 'To India?'

Karma shrugged. 'I really don't know,' he said. 'Maybe try and organise some sort of protest against the authorities.'

'Protest?' Tashi stiffened. She had heard reports of young Tibetans who had gone to extreme lengths to protest against Chinese human rights abuses – even to the point of suicide.

'Don't do something dangerous,' she whispered. 'You promise me?'

Karma smiled fondly at his sister. His eyes were two slits in the swollen flesh of his beaten face.

'I won't do anything crazy,' he said. 'I promise.'

He looked towards the sleeping shapes.

'Will you tell them?' he asked. 'Explain … if you can?'

'I'll try my best,' Tashi whispered. 'They'll be happy to know you are free.'

Karma leaned forward and embraced Tashi. Then he pulled his Dalai Lama portrait from his pocket and gave it to her.

'It's a bit bloodstained from the riot,' he said.

'It doesn't matter. I'll treasure it,' she said.

Karma smiled, then went and stood over his father, and his mother, chanting a Tibetan prayer for them in a barely audible whisper. He took out his little silver box of sacred beads and placed a jade bead into the sleeping hand of each of his parents.

'You've got one left haven't you?' Tashi smiled through her tears.

He nodded, showing her the precious bead before sealing it in the silver box and placing it in his pocket. Then he nodded one final time to his sister and slipped underneath the tent fabric into the dark Tibetan night.

Tashi lay there thinking. Would the family ever see Karma again? What would happen if the authorities caught him? She had heard stories about nomads, family men, that had been summoned for 'interviews' at military posts and were never seen again. No explanation. No forwarding address. No prisoner number. No mention of a trial. Just a terrible silence in which to try and rebuild a family torn apart.

Probably they were sent to prison camps, most Tibetans believed. Or forced to labour in the mines until they died. Either way they were gone; just another statistic in the roll call of thousands, possibly tens of thousands, of Tibetans whose lives had been disrupted or even ended by the Chinese since they had invaded the country.

Tashi curled up, pulling the thick blankets over her head, wanting to block out the world.

△

Early the next morning Tashi and her parents were taken to a nearby military garrison. They were placed in an interview room and left for a few hours without the offer of food or tea. Finally a military official entered, armed with a clipboard and pen.

'You are homeless?' the officer queried.

Tashi's father shook his head.

'Not at all,' he replied. 'We have our tent.'

'A tent?' the officer snorted derisively. 'Such temporary dwellings are not allowed. You will be much better off in a proper apartment in a town where you can all find work.'

'But ... '

'You are being rehoused,' the official interrupted.

'Everything is arranged. You will be taken to your new property tomorrow.'

'Everything is arranged ... ?' Tashi's father stammered. 'But how can it be arranged? We've only just been brought here.'

The official gave a secretive smile. Suddenly Tashi could not hold herself back.

'It's all part of a plan,' Tashi said. 'Blocking us from our grazing, condemning our herd, rehousing us in some horrible town. It's the same thing that's happening to thousands of nomad families.'

The official glared at Tashi and reached for a telephone.

'Hold your tongue,' he said. 'It only takes one call to make things a lot worse for you.'

The family were detained overnight in a concrete block next to the police station. Locked into a freezing room, they passed the night huddled up together on a mattress with just a flask of weak tea and some stale bread to eat.

Through the thin wall of the cell they could hear another family talking miserably about their fate.

'We're not the only ones,' Tashi's father said.

At 6 a.m. the door was flung open. A harsh voice barked at them.

'Come on! Quickly!'

They shuffled out to the yard. A military bus was waiting. They loaded their possessions on to the roof rack and took their seats alongside thirty other Tibetans.

'Do we get told where we are going?' one of the men asked.

None of the soldiers replied. The bus set off.

'I am being made to feel like a criminal,' Tashi's mother said.

Surly guards stood in the front of the bus, watching them for the whole journey.

'We are heading north,' Tashi's father observed.

From time to time the bus made 'comfort breaks', stopping for fifteen minutes so the occupants could collect stream water and answer calls of nature. Where the land offered no natural privacy the Tibetan women had no choice but to walk away from the bus and hold up a blanket as a screen.

'They could take us to a proper traveller's cafe if they wanted,' Tashi's mother said bitterly. 'This is all about embarrassing us.'

Tashi looked at the guards, sniggering behind their hands as they joked about the Tibetan women.

'It's almost as if they are *trying* to make us hate them,' she said.

'They don't have to try too hard,' her mother agreed.

Just before sunset the bus reached the crest of a high pass. The driver pulled in to a layby and turned off the engine. The occupants clambered off to stretch their weary limbs.

'This is where you are going to live,' an official said.

Tashi and her parents looked down into the valley where a sprawling new town was lying beneath a haze of yellow smog. Factories were spewing out smoke. Ugly high-rise blocks were being built in a dozen or more places. A massive mine was cut into the hillside directly above the town, endless rows of trucks shuttling along the highway that led to it.

'This is the future of Tibet!' the official said proudly.

Tashi thought it was the most depressing place she had ever seen.

The bus rattled down the hill and entered the town. Progress slowed to a crawl, heavy traffic jamming the streets as they passed through an industrial area.

Through the windows of the bus, Tashi could see factory workers walking to their night shifts. They looked worn out and exhausted, she thought, their pallid faces a total contrast to the sunburned complexions of the nomads on the plateau.

Occasionally the factory doors were open. Inside one she saw massive textile machines, clattering as they churned out countless metres of cloth. Through the windows of another unit Tashi was amazed to see hundreds of women working at desks. They were busy assembling things but she couldn't see what.

'Rubbish everywhere!' her mother exclaimed.

It was true that the streets were filthy.

Tashi felt tears prick her eyes.

△

One by one the families were dropped off, each one met by an official and guided towards faceless concrete apartment blocks. Tashi and her family were one of the last, taken from their seats and hurried off the bus into a dingy courtyard.

'You've got one minute to get your things off the roof rack!' the driver told them.

Tashi swarmed up the ladder and threw down their meagre possessions and their tent.

Just inside the building entrance was a small cubbyhole. Inside it lurked an obese janitor in a dirty vest. He sat back in his chair, watching a soap opera on a flickering black and white television, taking the occasional hostile glance at the newly arrived family.

'This is your new home,' the official said with a flourish of his arm. Tashi exchanged a horrified look with her father. The living room was not much more than a concrete shell, a dark and gloomy space with a glistening sheen of water running down one of the walls. The ceiling was streaked with a rust-coloured stain. The single pane of glass was dirty and cracked.

Tashi crossed to the window and stared out. The 'view' below was of a scrapyard in which half a dozen workers could be seen pulling apart fridges and washing machines. The rhythmic 'clang–clang–clang' of the yard's crushing machine pounded in her head.

'Can we choose another place?' Tashi's father asked.

The man snorted in a derisive way.

'Thousands of Tibetan families would love to have a residence like this,' he said. 'Show some gratitude.'

Tashi and her family began to carry in their possessions. A former nomad family living in the same block came down to help them.

The janitor let them take their pots and pans up to the flat. He also said nothing about the clothes and rugs. When it came to the bundles of the disassembled tent, however, he held his hand across the doorway.

'Where do you think you are going with all of this stuff?' he snapped.

'It's our tent,' Tashi's father explained. 'We'll be needing it again soon.'

'You can't take it in the building,' the man said. 'It's probably infested with lice and fleas.'

'It's not infested with anything!' Tashi told him. 'We clean it every spring.'

'Anyway there's no space,' the man said. 'You'll have to dump it.'

'Dump it?' Tashi's father stared at the man in astonishment. The man was casually suggesting the family should throw away its most precious possession.

'Or sell it. If you can.'

'We will never sell this tent!' Tashi's father exclaimed.

The confrontation turned into a stand-off; the janitor insisting that the ten huge bundles would not be allowed into the building, Tashi's father trying everything to persuade him to change his mind.

'I'll call the police if you want,' the janitor threatened finally. 'They know how to deal with your type.'

Tashi pulled her father back.

'Don't argue any more,' she urged him. 'It is useless. Better we find another place to store the tent.'

The family loaded the tent back on to the truck and paid the driver to take them into the centre of town. Asking around the market soon found a storeroom for hire.

'I smell rats,' Tashi's mother warned.

'We'll buy some plastic.'

The family wrapped the tent in multiple layers of plastic and paid to store it for three months. They returned to their new home on foot, walking through poorly lit streets choked with late night traffic.

'There are police stations everywhere,' Tashi's father complained. 'And they are spying on us!'

He pointed out the surveillance cameras positioned at every junction, on every street. Tashi stopped, staring up at one of the cameras. It swivelled on its pole, pointing directly at her.

'Come on!' her father pulled her away. 'We don't want to attract attention.'

They got a bit lost, reaching the accommodation block an hour later.

'Better we'd never found it again!' Tashi's mother exclaimed.

Tashi helped her mother and father to build a small shrine in the main room of their new home. Butter lamps were lit in front of holy figurines, incense was soon burning. It felt good to say a prayer for Karma.

They prepared the evening meal, an improvised stew of boiled barley flour with onions and peppers.

They placed a blanket on the unsurfaced floor and ate

together from the blackened cooking pot. It was the first time Tashi had ever known the family to be silent during a meal. Back on the plateau, after a day with the animals, there had never seemed a shortage of things to chat and laugh about.

After the meal Tashi's father crossed to the window and stared out into the night. The metallic beat of hammers continued to split the air in the yard below and Tashi wondered if the workers would be going all night.

'We are trapped,' her father said miserably. 'I fear we will never get out of this place.'

'We will,' Tashi's mother replied. 'We'll go crazy if we have to stay.'

Tashi saw her father's shoulders slump. The sharp tone in her mother's voice had cut into him. He shuffled to the sleeping room, looking small and defeated. The father she knew and loved, sitting tall and proud in the saddle of his favourite horse, seemed little more than a sad memory.

There was a sharp knock on the door. The same official that had brought them to the apartment stood awkwardly in the doorway.

'You will report for work to this place,' he said.

He handed Tashi a document. She saw a map printed on it.

'She's a child,' her father protested. 'Too young for work.'

The man poked his finger into Tashi's father's chest.

'Your family are already under scrutiny,' he said. 'Your son on the run from the law. Better you shut up or I'll send her to work with you in the mine.'

He handed Tashi's father a second map.

'There'll be punishments if you're late.'

Then he spun around and strode through the door.

Tashi went to her little sleeping place. It was more a cell or a cupboard than a bedroom. There was no heating and the temperature was low enough to set her teeth chattering. She pulled the blankets around her and tried to regain a little warmth.

Tomorrow she would be given a job. She wondered what on earth it would be. The only 'job' she had ever had was to care for her family's herd. She had no other skills. No other training. She remembered the hundreds of weary women sitting at the assembly lines in the factory. It seemed like a prison sentence.

Tashi uttered a prayer for Karma before she slept. More than anything she hoped her brother was OK. Would he come and find them?

Maybe he had already been caught.

Tashi shivered through the night, gripped by a horrible combination of cold and fear.

CHAPTER 4

Tashi's father accompanied her into town the next morning.

Close to the central square they came to a place lined with butchers' stalls. It was a busy scene of carnage, with dozens of shop owners cutting and sawing huge carcasses on wooden benches. In some places their wares were stacked in a tower two metres off the ground.

'So much meat!' Tashi exclaimed. 'I never saw so much meat in my life.'

'It's no cause for celebration,' her father reminded her. 'The only reason this place is overflowing with cheap meat is that all the yak herds are being forced from the land.'

Tashi stopped in her tracks, staring in dismay at the

teetering piles of gory flesh.

'These animals could be from our herd.'

Some of the pieces were still attached to a yak head or foot, a sick trophy to catch the eye of the passing shopper. Looking into the glazed eyes of some of these dead creatures she was struck by the contrast with the eyes of the animals she had tended as a young girl. Those intelligent eyes, filled with gentle patience and sometimes spiked, she had seen, with a mischievous sense of fun.

These cut up yaks belonged, she saw now, to families like her own. Families who had wandered the plateau as nomads for thousands of years. Many of them had been manoeuvred into situations where they had no choice but to slaughter their herds.

'It's all part of a grand scheme,' her father muttered angrily. 'Resettle all of us nomads in towns and work camps.'

Tashi could see the logic of the plan. All that extra meat fed the army of Chinese workers flooding into Tibet. And it solved the nomad 'problem' at the same time. She was beginning to realise how efficient the system was.

Her father was risking missing the bus to the mine, and so they split up, heading to different parts of town.

Tashi reported to the recruiting office as she had been ordered. She was relieved to find she was not alone.

A dozen other children of nomadic families were also waiting to be given official jobs. They sat together in a stark concrete waiting room, whispering dark rumours to each other about what the authorities might require them to do.

'They send the pretty girls away to Beijing or Shanghai,' one girl told her in a terrified whisper. 'Then they're never seen again.'

Tashi wasn't sure she believed her but the warning didn't help. Perhaps it was one of those urban myths, Tashi hoped; one of those rumours that creates uncertainty and fear.

For two hours they sat with nothing to do except read the public information posters on the wall. Most were laying down strict laws about drugs and gambling. But others were more in the way of propaganda, forbidding public gatherings or demonstrations.

Finally a uniformed official entered the room. He consulted a clipboard for a few seconds then stared at the Tibetan youths in evident dislike.

'You will kill rats,' he said.

Tashi looked at the government man in amazement. She had never killed a rat in her life. The nomad children burst into laughter and began to chat in bewilderment.

'It is not a joke,' the man snapped irritably. 'You will kill thousands of rats. And then you will kill thousands more.'

The 'rats', it soon turned out, were not really rats at all. They were pika, grass-eating mammals of the plateau, targeted for extermination under a new environmental law which had been drafted from Beijing.

Tashi had always been fond of pika; they were halfway between a rabbit and a gerbil – intelligent creatures she had been familiar with all her life. They were smart, Tashi knew; instead of hibernating through the winter, they built underground food stores of grass seeds. Sometimes as a child she had joined other nomad children, digging up the burrows to see how they were constructed. In the depths were the food stores and the crèches for the pika young. It was surprisingly well organised and clean.

It was true that pika were widespread. But they were part of the ecosystem: food for the wolves, the bears, the foxes, the hawks and kestrels. Virtually everything ate pika, Tashi knew. What would happen if the pika were gone was something she could not contemplate, yet to the authorities the creatures were public enemy number one. Pika cause the grasslands to wither and dry, their reports said. They are breeding out of control, digging millions of burrows, ravaging crops and laying vast tracts of the Tibetan plateau bare. They spread plague, harbour fleas. Pika are the enemy – they must be destroyed.

Tashi and the other children were ordered to report to a depot the following morning. They returned home to their government housing blocks in a gloomy state of mind.

'Do you have a job?' Tashi's father asked her.

'Kind of,' she replied. She felt her cheeks flush. Her father waited for more information but Tashi strode stony-faced to her room without saying more. Killing pika was just about the worst job she could think of.

△

At daybreak she walked across town with two of her new friends. They found the depot right on the outskirts, next to an abattoir that pumped out noxious grey smoke.

They were issued with plastic gloves and a face mask and bundled on to the back of an open truck. A two-hour drive followed, bouncing around in the metal box as the vehicle lumbered up a potholed track on to a wild grassland area. There were no tents visible and the land was dusty and dry. Plastic sacks of grain were offloaded from another vehicle. Each was marked with a skull and crossbones symbol.

'This is special grain,' the official told them, 'coated with a poison to kill the rats. Two handfuls in each rat hole will be enough.'

The children exchanged glances. There were thousands of pika burrows dotted around this area of grassland. The task would be a backbreaking one.

'Pick up these baskets and fill them with grain,' he urged. The bamboo baskets were massive and badly worn out. Bits of broken bamboo were sticking like knife points from the weave. None of the children moved.

'Come on! We haven't got all day! There's a quota to fill!'

A few of the children walked uncertainly across. They slipped the leather straps over their shoulders and moved over to the store where two workers slit open the plastic sacks and poured the contents directly into the baskets. Tashi winced as she saw a cloud of dust swirl around her friends' heads.

'Isn't that dangerous?' one of the other children asked. 'If it's a poison they shouldn't be breathing it, right?'

'It's harmless to humans,' the supervisor snapped.

Tashi couldn't help noticing that he kept as far away from the toxin as he could.

'I don't want to kill pika,' Tashi blurted out.

The supervisor placed himself squarely in front of her. Tashi felt the hairs on the back of her neck prickle as his fish-cold eyes locked on to hers.

'You can always be sent to a correction centre if you

prefer?' he sneered.

Tashi shivered. She had heard spine-chilling tales of such 'correction centres', labour camps in which Tibetans were forced to produce written confessions of their 'faults' whilst labouring ten hours a day. Smashing up rocks into tiny pieces for road gravel was a favourite task for such 'criminals'.

'Well?' the supervisor snapped.

Tashi bit her lip. She thought about running away, sprinting across the grassland and escaping from these horrible people. But she knew her mother and father could be punished. She had to stay and see this through.

'That's better,' the supervisor stroked her head in a patronising fashion. 'Come and get your load.'

Tashi followed him to the pile of grain sacks and was issued with a basket. On the side of the sacks she read the words *Botulinum Toxin*. She had never heard of this particular poison but she memorised the words anyway.

Botulinum Toxin. What did it do? She wondered. How would it act on the pika? Would it kill them quickly, without pain? Or was it a slow death? Tashi hated to think of so many thousands of creatures suffering and dying.

A whistle blew. It was time to get to work. Each of the children on their own. There were plenty of pika to be seen and the burrows were literally everywhere.

Tashi found the work was repetitive and painful. Bending down to place the poisoned grain into the pika burrows, the heavy load biting into her spine.

Each time the basket was empty she returned to the truck. The driver refilled it with fresh poison and the supervisor pointed out a new area of grassland to work in. She did this six times, getting ever further away from the truck as she pushed away from the road.

Finally she was out of sight of the organisers and could take some time out. She put down the basket and lay back on the cool grass, staring up at the azure sky and letting her mind slip away.

Her daydream took her back to childhood years, when her family could move freely. She remembered every camp, the fun of bathing in fast-flowing meltwater rivers, the dramas of yaks that went astray for days on end and had to be tracked by the dogs, the birds of prey that were tamed by her grandfather and taught to hunt hares.

Tashi wondered if she would ever live in a tent again. Or was that part of her life over for good?

△

A siren was blasted at lunchtime and the hungry children gathered by the truck. A pot of cold rice was produced and they crouched round it on their haunches, eating with their bare hands. Green tea was handed out in plastic cups.

'I feel dizzy,' someone muttered. Tashi wondered if the poison was beginning to take effect.

They gulped down the rice and tea and all too soon the supervisor was yelling at them:

'No time for lazing! We're moving to the next location.'

The team was loaded back into the truck and the vehicles lurched off. They travelled down a small track, passing several huge mines along the way. These complexes were busy eating away big chunks of hillsides, thousands of tons of rock being crushed in machines that could be heard roaring several kilometres distant.

Explosions split the air. Billowing clouds of dust spewed from the mines, darkening the sky.

'What are they digging for?' Tashi asked.

'Gold,' came a reply. 'It gets sent to Beijing.'

After the mines came a high col, and a descent into a region of pretty valleys. It was perfect pika habitat, Tashi knew, but she soon learned that the creatures in this area had already had their burrows laced.

'This is a zone they've already poisoned,' one of the other children exclaimed. 'I was working here the other week.'

Tashi wrinkled her nose as a pungent smell reached her.

The stench of decomposition was faint but identifiable. Tashi felt bile rise in her throat as the scent of rotting pika bodies hit her.

The trucks stopped. The supervisor jumped out.

'Ten minutes,' he told them. 'I need to check things here.'

Men were wandering about the grassland, holding long sticks. They were dressed in identical grey overalls and one of the children muttered that they might be prisoners. They were retrieving the rotting corpses of the dead pika from the burrows and piling them up by the side of the road.

'They burn the bodies,' someone said. 'Stop the other creatures eating them.'

Tashi thought about this, wondering how efficient the system was. Did they really manage to find every dead pika? What if a fox or an eagle ate one of the poisoned animals? Would it also get sick and die?

She looked around, her heart sagging as she realised there was no life in any direction. Not a single songbird, not a hawk in the sky. Even the grasshoppers that usually chirped incessantly were quiet.

The land was dead. Slaughtering the pika seemed to have upset a natural balance. Nature had fled.

By the time they were delivered back to the town the

children were utterly exhausted. Burned by the sun and feeling rather sick, Tashi walked back to the concrete block that was now her home. Her parents greeted her with loving embraces and fed her warm barley soup and sweet *momos* of honey.

'Did they treat you well?' her father asked.

Tashi nodded her head. She didn't want to worry her parents.

Tashi went to her sleeping cubicle. At dawn the next morning the whole process would be repeated again. She rested her head on her pillow, wondering in the final moments of the day what she could do to break free from this horrible work. Was there a way out? How long would she have to spend poisoning the pika?

She was bone-tired but could not sleep. The thought of all those creatures eating the grain and feeding it to their young was more than she could bear. A terrible guilt washed over her.

△

As the days turned into weeks and she continued to work with the toxin, Tashi felt her body weakening. Getting out of bed became a slow process, stretching her aching muscles and rubbing her legs vigorously to coax them into life.

One day she felt so faint she had to pause on the way to work, reaching out to steady herself against a nearby wall.

'I'm seeing double,' she told her friend.

'That's strange. I'm the same.'

'My throat has stopped working properly,' another worker complained. 'I can hardly swallow food.'

One boy told how his digestive system had locked up in a terrible bout of constipation.

'We should get on to the internet,' he suggested. 'Maybe we can discover what this poison is doing to us. There's a man I heard about who knows how to get round the censorship.'

Tashi joined her friend after work and they took a bus across town. He took her to a basement beneath a block of flats and at the door they buzzed a special code.

A nervy-looking guy with shoulder length hair opened the door a crack, then, after a brief interrogation to satisfy himself they weren't government spies, he let them in.

'Just call me Mouse,' said the computer buff. 'It's ten yuan an hour.'

He showed them into his computer den, a sweltering box room with blacked-out windows and a lingering smell of egg noodles.

'Just tell me what you want to know,' Mouse said. 'I can hack most things.'

'Hack? What does it mean?' Tashi asked.

'The Chinese government stop people looking at stuff on the internet,' the guy explained. 'Google, Facebook, Twitter. They block them all.'

'Why?'

Tashi's friend and Mouse shared a knowing look. Tashi felt her cheeks redden, she knew she was naive about these things.

'When people rise up against a government they often do it using social media,' her friend said. 'That's what happened when the people of the Arabic world rebelled against the dictators who ruled Tunisia and Egypt.'

'You think the Chinese government is frightened of their own *people*?' Tashi asked.

Mouse laughed. 'You bet they are! Now take a seat.'

It was strangely thrilling for Tashi to be sitting in front of a computer terminal for the first time in her life.

'We want to find out about Botulinum Toxin,' her friend said.

Mouse googled the poison and quickly found information about it. Tashi was astonished how fast the process was.

'I've got a list of symptoms this stuff can cause,' he said.

Mouse printed it out. Virtually every single one of the health problems Tashi and her friends had been experiencing was there in black and white.

'It's conclusive,' her friend said. 'At least we know for sure.'

'You got fifty minutes left,' Mouse said. 'Any more requests? Or I can show you the Tiananmen Square hacks I pulled off yesterday if you like?'

'Tiananmen Square?' Tashi frowned. 'What's that?'

'It's a massive demonstration we're not supposed to know about,' her friend told her. 'The moment when the people of China almost brought down their own government.'

'Really?'

'It's totally censored by Beijing,' Mouse added. 'It's taken me six months to get round the blocks.'

He tapped feverishly at the keyboard.

'This is a BBC News report of the early stages,' he said, turning the screen to face them.

The image flickered magically into life. Thousands of Chinese protestors were waving banners and singing in a huge square.

'So many people,' Tashi said in wonder. 'What do they all want?'

'Change. Freedom to live their lives without interruption and control by the government.'

'Old people, young people. Everyone is there!' her friend said.

'And the soldiers are joining them!' Tashi added. The footage showed young military men, smiling shyly at the camera as they linked arms with the protestors.

'These were the first couple of days,' Mouse said. 'But things went sour pretty quickly once the government saw that they were losing control.'

He tapped more words into the search box.

Tashi frowned as she saw demonstrators running in the next clip. Canisters of white smoke were going off in the video, soldiers were beating people with their batons. Water cannons were directed at the panicking masses. Tashi got the impression of total chaos.

Then the camera swung towards a group of soldiers. They looked astonishingly young. A student protestor wearing a bandana and looking little more than sixteen years old yelled something towards them and an officer barked a command. One of the young soldiers pulled out a gun.

And shot the protestor through the head.

Tashi felt her chest constrict. Her breathing became rapid and her head began to spin.

'Let me see that again,' Tashi said.

Mouse ran the clip once more.

'Can you stop the image when I say?' Tashi asked.

'Sure.'

Tashi got Mouse to stop the video so she could get a good look at the young soldier's face. The image was crystal clear. He was a lot younger than he looked now but there was no doubt.

'I know that person,' she said. 'His name is Chen.'

△

That night Tashi found herself sweating in her sheets. Her breath became short; she was suffering from asthma for the first time in her life.

The video footage of the Tiananmen Square incident was playing over and over in her mind. Chen shooting that student. An unarmed boy. Straight through the forehead.

The man that Karma had fought back against was already a killer.

It was the speed at which he obeyed the order from his officer. The unquestioning way he had just pulled out his pistol and killed a boy virtually his own age. Like a robot. Like a machine. Tashi could not get those pictures out of her mind. And it made her even more fearful for her brother.

Work continued, the poisoning campaign rolled on for month after month until finally it was impossible for Tashi to continue to hide the effects from her parents.

'Your skin is looking terrible,' her mother told her. 'And your eyes are bloodshot all the time. Are you sick, Tashi?'

But Tashi still kept the toxin work secret. When they asked what she was doing she replied she was 'working in the fields'. It was partly true, but Tashi felt terrible to be hiding the true nature of her work from them.

More time passed. Then came the throat problems. A hacking cough which just would not clear up. One day after breakfast her mother took her aside.

'I can't remember the last time you were well,' she said tenderly. 'What is happening to you Tashi?'

'Nothing,' she sniffed. 'Just under the weather that's all.'

'It's the work, isn't it?' her father demanded. 'What are they doing to you?'

Tashi was tired of keeping her secret. She told them the whole story, watching their expressions darken thunderously as the tale unfolded.

'They are not just poisoning the pika,' her father said. 'They're poisoning you too.'

Tashi's father walked with her to the work depot the next morning, determined to have it out with the supervisor. Tashi stood with her heart tripping as the boss looked up to see who had barged into his office.

'What are you doing to my daughter?' her father demanded. 'Look how sick she has become. Why do you force her to handle poisons every day?'

'We certainly do not,' the supervisor snapped. 'We only distribute such toxins by aircraft. We drop them safely from the air so that no one has to handle them.'

Tashi felt her mouth fall open. This official was telling a bare-faced lie.

'Then how do you explain her sickness?' Tashi's father asked.

'She probably caught something from one of the other workers,' he suggested. 'There are many chronic diseases amongst the local population.'

'My daughter hardly had a day sick in her life,' Tashi's father objected. 'Only when she came under your control did she become ill.'

The supervisor rose.

'This interview is over,' he snapped.

He showed them abruptly to the door.

'I think he's corrupt,' Tashi's father said as they walked the streets towards home. 'He's taken the money for the aircraft and kept it for himself.'

'Probably,' Tashi said. 'He does drive an expensive car.'

'We need to get you out of this work,' her father continued.

'Need to get you out of this place entirely if we can.'

By the light of a paraffin lamp the family talked late into the night. The conversation centred on two themes: how to escape their predicament. And how to get Karma back into their lives.

△

'We could trek to India,' Tashi's mother proposed. 'Join the Dalai Lama's community in Dharamsala. Maybe Karma is already there.'

Tashi's father smiled sadly. He peeled an egg of its shell and passed it to Tashi.

'Leave our homeland?' he questioned. 'You know we'll never be allowed back.'

'There's no guarantees we'd make it across the mountains,' Tashi said. 'The passes are high, guarded by troops.'

'We'd be living off charity for the rest of our lives,' her father added. 'I've heard there's no work there.'

'Maybe things would be better in Lhasa?' Tashi wondered. 'Perhaps they don't hassle people as much there.'

'And work in a factory?' her father said. 'At least here we can see mountains, watch the rivers flow.'

'And get poisoned,' her mother added. 'Don't forget that.'

The room went quiet. Tashi felt despondent. For a while

no one said anything. Then they went to their small family shrine and prayed together for a while. Tashi brought out her bloodstained photograph of the Dalai Lama, thinking intently about Karma and wondering for the thousandth time where her brother could be.

Her mother prepared more yak butter tea, warming some flatbread on the stove. Finally her father spoke:

'We should go to the sacred lake of Lhamo La-tso,' he said. 'We will find the answer there.'

'How will a lake help us?' Tashi asked. She had never heard of the place.

'It can give visions of the future. It's to the south of Lhasa,' her father continued.

Tashi's mother nodded enthusiastically. 'When the Regents were looking for clues to divine where the next Dalai Lama could be found, they went to Lhamo La-tso.'

'They prayed for many days, then saw letters in the waters,' her father continued. 'Other clues about a building with turquoise tiles.'

'When they found the young boy all the clues fell into place,' her mother said. 'They would never have found him without that vision.'

Tashi smiled. Her parents' faith in the power of the lake was touching, but she found it hard to think things could be that simple.

'You don't believe us?' her mother said.

'Perhaps it can show a vision for the Dalai Lama,' she answered slowly. 'But we are not important like him.'

'The lake will show us the way,' her father insisted. 'It might even help us to get Karma back. We should go as soon as possible.'

Tashi signed in sick so that she and her father could set out one week later on the bus journey to the lake. Getting travel papers had proved tricky; bribes were necessary to persuade officials to issue the permit. The trip was hard going, the roads dusty and hot. In total it was twenty hours travelling.

Tashi lost count of the police checkpoints. Roadblocks seemed to be everywhere and they were questioned frequently by the young police recruits who climbed on board the coach.

'Where are you going?' they demanded. 'What is the purpose of your journey?'

'Pilgrimage,' Tashi's father replied serenely. The word normally provoked a sneer from the guards and they would move on to the next traveller.

'Why are they so suspicious of us?' Tashi whispered to her father. 'What exactly do they think we're doing wrong?'

'Harassment,' he replied. 'The authorities don't like the thought of Tibetans travelling freely around their own country.'

Tashi's small travelling bag was searched three times. She blushed as the young guards laughed at her meagre possessions. At one of the checkpoints a guard pulled her hairbrush from the bag and played the fool with it, brushing imaginary locks. Tashi snatched the brush back and quickly zipped the bag up.

'Just for fun!' the guard snapped. He pinched Tashi's cheek hard, his eyes suddenly cold. 'You should learn how to take a joke.'

Tashi's father gripped her hand tightly as a warning not to retaliate.

A final overnight bus brought them to their destination. Tashi was dozing when the lake came into view at dawn.

'Wake up!' her father urged. 'We've arrived.'

Tashi blinked sleep from her eyes and stumbled stiffly out of the bus. The vehicle pulled away, the rumble of the engine gradually diminishing to be replaced by the gentle play of wind across the lake.

'Am I still dreaming?' Tashi said in wonder. Her father smiled contentedly.

The lake was exquisite, the water such a vivid tone of

saturated blue it felt like it was filled with melted lapis lazuli. The shores were ringed with snow-capped mountains.

They walked down to the water's edge, to a small shingle beach. Pilgrims had stacked stones to form cairns and there were many colourful strings of prayer flags fluttering in the breeze.

'Now you see?' Tashi's father gestured proudly, as if he had created the lake himself.

Tashi did see. It was beautiful, by far the most spectacular place the young Tibetan girl had ever seen.

A falcon let out an eerie cry above them. Golden rays of light washed across the scene as the sun rose. Small waves rippled across the lake as a flurry of wind raced to the east. It was mystical, Tashi felt, filled with irresistible magic.

'And the vision?' she whispered.

Her father laughed. 'Not so fast, it's not like switching on a television. But it will come, you can be sure of that.'

CHAPTER 5

They walked to a nearby hamlet and paid for a simple room. A hearty breakfast of steamed *momos* followed, tiny dumplings stuffed with spiced pork. The meal was eaten in the company of other pilgrims from far-flung corners of Tibet. Tashi enjoyed the little details of clothing and jewellery that gave clues as to where they came from.

A friendly discussion began around the table. Tibetans will strike up a conversation with anyone and the pilgrims were keen to share their stories.

Two of the pilgrims – like Tashi and her father – were hoping to see personal visions; others wished to pay their respects to the lake which many years earlier had showed the Regents of Tibet where they could find a two-year-old boy who lived far to the east: Tenzin Gyatso, the fourteenth Dalai Lama. His connection to the lake gave it a very special power in the eyes of all Tibetans.

'What shall we do tomorrow?' Tashi asked her father as they prepared to sleep.

'Visit the local temples,' he replied. 'And pray by the lake.'

His proposal didn't just cover the following day, it was the pattern for each of the next three days. Mornings in the smoky shrines, adding molten butter to the lamps that glimmered with sacred fire. Afternoons kneeling at the blustery shore of the lake, praying fervently and keeping watch for anything that could be interpreted as a sign.

They made many firm friends but no vision presented itself. Tashi found herself becoming impatient, complaining out loud about the long hours they were spending by the water's edge, her restlessness finally provoking her father to a response.

'Nothing will happen unless we are both calm,' he told her strictly. 'There must be no anxiety in our hearts.'

Tashi tried to take his advice but it wasn't easy. Other pilgrims were announcing the wonders they had witnessed on a daily basis yet for Tashi and her father … nothing.

On their final day at the sacred lake, Tashi and her father decided to take a walk around the shore. There was a village about ten kilometres away which would make a good objective for a there-and-back trek.

They left the lodging house at first light, picking a way along the rocky shoreline and keeping a careful eye on the lake for any strange waves or reflections. There was little conversation between them. The failure of the expedition so far had left them both a little depressed and there was a real sense of anti-climax about the journey.

'It's going to be bad for Mum if we have to tell her we've failed,' Tashi said. 'We've spent plenty of money apart from anything else.'

'There is still time,' her father insisted. 'Something might yet happen.'

Tashi had to smile at her father's optimism.

Just before noon they reached their destination, a small settlement of about a hundred inhabitants. They begged some drinking water from a friendly mechanic, took a look around the dusty streets, and got into a confrontation with a pack of not-so-friendly local dogs intent on running them out of town.

They retreated to the lake shore to have a picnic lunch, placing a cloth on the stony ground and laying out boiled eggs, cheese and dried yak meat. The day was hot and humid, the atmosphere heavy with the threat of a thunderstorm.

Soon they heard the sound of laughter and a dozen children came down to the lakeside to play.

Tashi and her father watched the children as they ate their lunch. Some of the bolder ones had gone in for a swim. One of them had pushed out from the shore with a small plastic inflatable – a red and yellow dragon. He looked confident as he kicked his legs out behind him. The boy was about eight, Tashi guessed.

Suddenly the mood changed. The other children started throwing small stones at the boy, taunting him and calling names.

'Leave him alone!' Tashi called.

For a moment she thought to intervene. But the child kicked out of range of the stones and things quietened down.

Tashi and her father finished their lunch and lay back on the rug to take a rest. No sooner had Tashi closed her eyes than a small hand tugged at her wrist.

'Wake up, miss. Wake up!'

Tashi sat up. A young girl was standing there, a troubled expression on her face.

'Look!' she pointed towards the lake.

The boy had floated far from the shore, still clutching his dragon inflatable. He was kicking wildly, going round in circles.

'Help!' he cried out. 'Help please!'

'What's his problem?' Tashi asked.

'The float has a leak. He can't swim!'

△

Tashi got quickly to her feet, blinking in surprise as she saw how quickly the weather had changed: the placid waters of early morning had been whipped away by the wind. Now there were waves, spitting up spray. The sun was suddenly blanked out by dark cloud. Thunder rolled across the mountains.

Tashi ran down to the lakeside. Her father joined her. There were no other adults around so she took off her fleece and her boots.

'What are you doing?' her father asked in astonishment.

'That boy is in trouble,' she replied.

The children chattered excitedly as Tashi removed her clothes. The boy was still calling, his voice increasingly thin and desperate.

'It's sinking! Help me!'

Tashi plunged into the lake, dressed in her underclothes, gasping as the freezing waters embraced her. Fifty strokes took her out to the inflatable dragon. Tashi had always been a strong swimmer. She felt calm and in control. Her body warmed as her muscles tuned into the swim.

By the time she reached the boy he was wild-eyed and desperate. He grabbed Tashi's arm, astonishing force in his fingers.

'C … c … cold,' he stuttered. Tashi saw that his lips were already blue.

The dragon was two-thirds deflated. Air was hissing out of a small pinhole; there was barely enough pressure to support the boy's weight. Waves were cresting over his head. He was swallowing water, beginning to choke.

Tashi half pushed the inflatable toy, half towed it towards the shore. The wind was against her now, making it quite a struggle, but she kicked out hard with her legs as the boy cried for his mother.

Five metres from safety the plastic dragon finally sank.

'Put your hands on my shoulders,' Tashi told the boy.

They got to the shore, but the spot was not an easy place to exit the lake. There was a small embankment and the waves were lapping aggressively against it. After a few false starts the boy was dragged awkwardly up the bank by the other children. Tashi reached for her father and got a hand out.

A woman ran down from the village, screaming for her son. When she saw that he was safe she wrapped him in her shawl and carried him away without so much as a word of thanks to Tashi.

'There's gratitude!' her father said.

Tashi shivered. The wind was biting now.

'Dry yourself with the fleece,' her father told her. Tashi dried herself as best as she could then slipped on her clothes.

Tashi's father put his arm around her shoulders.

'Come on. We need to get you back to the hostel.'

Tashi pulled away, turning back to the lake.

'And the vision?' she asked. 'We've been here three days and nothing's happened.'

Her father sighed. They stood side by side, looking out across the wind-tossed waves of the lake. The storm had intensified, a brooding mass of cloud was now hanging low over the water. Rain was falling on the far side of the lake.

'Maybe it was too much to ask,' he said sadly. 'Perhaps we are not worthy.'

Tashi screwed up her eyes, trying to find a shape amongst the clouds, anything out of the ordinary. Then she tried the same trick on the water, blurring her vision so that the reflected clouds became distorted.

Nothing.

Tashi felt the cold biting hard. She needed to get warm soon. Then she hesitated. She saw something … an item of clothing was bobbing up and down in the choppy waves. It was the boy's T-shirt. As the other children had pulled him out of the water it must have been ripped off his back. Now the garment was floating in the lake, suspended just beneath the surface, the printed front facing upwards. The image was a graphic representation of a mountain, beneath it the caption:

EVEREST 8848

The effect was mesmerising. Magnified by refraction, the movement of the crystal clear water made it seem like the mountain on the T-shirt was rippling, dancing. At that moment a blaze of sunlight suddenly burst through the storm clouds, a single ray painting the garment with brilliant light.

Tashi turned to her father. Her eyes were shining, the cold forgotten.

'That's it,' she said. 'That's our sign.'

△

Tashi and her father rushed back to their lodging house, keen to tell their fellow pilgrims about the vision. In return they got a lot of information, including advice from a man who had been on a three-month pilgrimage to the Rongbuk monastery at the very foot of Everest.

'There is a community of Tibetans working at Everest Base Camp,' the pilgrim told them. 'They run the yak transport taking the expedition equipment up to the mountain.'

Tashi smiled at her father. Running yaks was second nature to them.

'Is there plenty of work?' Tashi asked. 'Do you think we would get an opportunity there?'

'There are new people arriving every year,' the man said. 'But the work is so hard that many quit. The journey up the glacier takes three or four days and goes to the very limit of what the yaks can manage.'

'My cousin tried it one year,' another pilgrim said. 'He lasted three weeks and ended up losing fingers to frostbite.'

'It's cold up there,' the first man nodded, shuddering with the memory. 'Cold like you cannot imagine.'

Tashi felt a tingle of excitement. Working at Everest Base Camp sounded exotic and challenging.

'There is no proper trail,' the man warned. 'Much of the journey is on ice. Yaks are lost almost every day, falling in crevasses, dying of exhaustion.'

'What about the money?' Tashi's father asked. 'Is the pay good?'

'I believe so,' the man replied. 'Most of the teams up

there are Westerners. They pay a bonus if their stuff arrives safely.'

His words fired off strange emotions in Tashi. To work at Base Camp would mean contact with foreigners. Tashi had never spoken to anyone from outside of Tibet or China. She had seen the occasional tourist group, trundling at speed across the plateau in their minibuses and Toyota 4x4s.

But to actually *speak* with one … It was an outrageous and curious thought.

Tashi and her father arrived home two days later, fired with determination to follow up on the vision. Tashi had feared her mother might be against the idea. Going to work at Everest Base Camp would immerse them in the wildest and coldest region of Tibet, living at an altitude of almost six thousand metres. But she was enthusiastic from the start:

'The sooner the better,' her mother exclaimed. 'We need to get out of this town, out of this situation.'

Best of all, Tashi's father had a friend who could help them to make some contacts. His name was Tenzin, a driver with a road construction team. He was working on a highway project just twenty miles from Everest Base Camp. He promised to put out feelers to see if the family could find work.

Three weeks later he called round to share his news.

'I spoke to my friends,' he told Tashi and her parents. 'And they've agreed to help you.'

Tashi beamed at her father. Tibetan solidarity had come good just as she had hoped. The plan was coming together.

'There are markets where you can buy yaks,' Tenzin told them. 'You'll have to pay for forged papers as well.'

'No problem,' Tashi's father agreed.

'It can be deadly up there,' Tenzin warned. 'Three yak drivers have been killed by avalanche in the last couple of years.'

Tashi's father made contact with a local fixer, a man who was known to help Tibetans go secretly into exile in India and Nepal. The man had a four-wheel-drive truck and an encyclopaedic knowledge of the lonely back roads and tracks which would avoid police checkpoints.

'You understand that you cannot come back,' the fixer said. 'The authorities will imprison you for years if you show your faces in this town again.'

'We've thought it through,' Tashi's father said. 'Living here under the Chinese is the same as a prison sentence anyway.'

A sum was agreed. The family tent was retrieved from the storeroom at the market.

Five days later, on the next moonless night, Tashi and her family were spirited away from the mining town. Their 3 a.m. departure was not noticed.

By the time they were missed, they would be hundreds of kilometres away, their disappearance written off as another Tibetan family gone into exile, never to return.

Tashi watched the fading lights of the mining town through the back window of the truck. She made a promise to herself. Whatever happened she would never be a slave again.

For the first time in a year she felt free.

△

Thirty hours later the clandestine journey was over. The truck revved up the final steep mountain road and the family got their first view of their destination.

Tashi's father was the first out of the cab. He jumped down and she heard him give a quiet exclamation of delight.

'What a place!'

Tashi climbed down to join him, feeling a shudder of excitement run through her body.

The scene in front of her was even more impressive than she had imagined. In her mind she had pictured that Base Camp might be a couple of dozen tents and an equal number of yaks.

Now she saw so many tents she could hardly count them, hundreds upon hundreds of domes, dotted across the valley in a riot of vivid yellows, reds and greens. Climbers were hard at work amongst their temporary homes, sorting out piles of climbing equipment, coiling endless kilometres of ropes. On the grazing area, next to a collection of Tibetan nomads' tents, was a small army of yaks.

'It's like a city,' Tashi said in wonder.

'So many people want to climb this mountain?' Tashi's mother asked in amazement.

To the left of the expedition area a spectacular monastery hugged the valley walls.

'The Rongbuk. One of the most ancient religious centres in Tibet,' her father said with satisfaction. 'Later we will go and pray there.'

They unloaded their possessions and Tashi's father announced he would go off to find the contact who had promised to help them.

Tashi and her mother took the opportunity to wander around the camp, enjoying the chaos of the scene, eavesdropping on more foreign languages than they could have imagined existed.

'It's the start of the season,' Tashi realised as they saw stack after stack of newly arrived supplies. 'We've arrived at exactly the right moment.'

Above all there was a delicious energy to the scene. A sense of purpose in the way the climbers moved amongst the tents, from the laughter and the chat a feeling of community which was entirely unexpected.

'I think we're going to like this place,' her mother said.

'Like it?' Tashi smiled. 'We're going to love it!'

Tashi's father had found the chief yak herder, a wise-looking old nomad without a single tooth in his head. He welcomed them all warmly and showed them to a vacant patch of ground where they could pitch their tent. There wasn't much grazing, but it was flat and dry.

Tashi spotted a circular area where the rocks had been cleared. A tent had been pitched in the same place quite recently.

'What happened to the last people who stayed here?' Tashi asked.

'Oh,' the chief replied. 'There was a storm and the man got lost. He was out on the glacier for two days in this blizzard and we couldn't find him … '

He didn't need to say more. Two days lost on the glacier was a death sentence for sure.

The chief's tale was a sombre reminder of the risks the family would face but Tashi soon forgot about the story as they put up the family tent. It was a nostalgic experience for them. Every wooden strut felt like an old friend. Every piece of fabric was familiar to the touch.

'Can I give you some help?' said a voice.

Tashi whipped round. Her mother gasped.

A figure was standing before them, dressed in a Western climber's fleece and trekking trousers. He was burned by the sun, a little taller and stronger than before.

'Karma?' Tashi's heart pounded in her chest. She thought for a moment that she might be seeing a ghost.

Then he smiled and she knew for sure.

'Karma!'

Tashi ran to her brother and wrapped her arms around him. Next moment her parents were joining in, the four of them holding each other tight in a joyful reunion that had the people around them laughing with pleasure.

'I prayed so hard,' Karma said. 'I never doubted that you would come.'

'Let's finish the tent,' their father said, finally. 'Then we can share our news.'

Karma and Tashi were in heaven, running around happily, helping to erect their family home.

Two neighbours came to welcome them, cheerful nomad women bearing gifts of barley and meat.

The family ate a good meal together that night as Karma told his story.

'I had a hard time the first winter,' he told them. 'I was working in an illegal mine in the mountains of the East. I injured my hand and got sacked with no pay.'

Tashi reached for Karma's hand and saw the jagged scar stretching right across the back of it.

'Then I heard about this work helping out with the yaks at Base Camp and thought it sounded all right. I haven't been able to buy my own animals but it's really OK up here.'

'We've got the money for three yaks,' their father said. 'Is there enough work?'

'Definitely,' Karma replied. 'More and more expeditions come every year.'

After the meal the family went to pray at the Rongbuk monastery.

Tashi kneeled next to Karma, filled with pure joy to have her younger brother back by her side. The sign at the lake had been more than just a pointer to a new future, she realised now; it had provided the pathway to reunite the family.

That night, safe in the tent with the people she loved around her, Tashi felt she had been truly blessed.

△

Word went out. The family were in the market for pack animals. Plenty of offers came in, all of them boasting of wonderful creatures in the peak of health. Closer inspection revealed the truth: the yaks for sale were ancient and sometimes lame. Tashi smiled every time she heard a trader singing the praises of an exhausted old beast.

Her family had spent their entire lives working with these animals. The idea that they could be conned into buying a dud was laughable.

Finally, some days later, they travelled to the monthly market at the town of Tingri. Nomads from all over the plateau came to this famous trading place and, sure enough, it wasn't long before they had spotted three animals for sale.

'It's a bit more money than we expected,' her father said after some negotiations. 'But they'll give us five years of service if we treat them right.'

A deal was struck and Tashi's father handed over the cash. Tashi knew it was the last of the family savings. Everything would depend on these yaks.

If things didn't work out here at Everest Base Camp there was only one last option in front of them: exile. Leaving Tibet for good. The very last thing that any of them wanted. They had to make this work.

The first days with their new yak team were filled with a thousand tasks. Getting to know the quirks of each animal was vital.

'We'll take them on a test trek,' their father said.

They loaded a small weight on to each yak and took them on a ten-kilometre round trip up the glacier. The ice was starting to thaw with the spring melt and the trails were slippery and dangerous.

For Karma it was business as usual. He had worked on the glacier for more than a year, but Tashi only now began to appreciate just how tough the transport work was going to be for the beasts and themselves.

Her father was also on a steep learning curve.

'There's nothing to breathe,' he complained.

He stopped frequently to rest, coughing hard and wheezing in the thin air. The altitude was more of a problem than Tashi had imagined. They were almost two thousand metres higher here than the height they had previously lived at.

'It's his lungs,' Karma said. 'I'm not sure he can handle it.'

Their father was grey in the face and wobbly on his feet by the time they got back from the test trek.

'We only did a quarter of the trek up to the North Col camp,' Karma said quietly to Tashi. 'And it almost finished him.'

Tashi nodded sadly.

'It's going to be down to you and me,' she said. 'I don't think Father's going to be well enough to do the big treks.'

Karma agreed. He had already worked it out.

Tashi realised very quickly that she would have to speak English to be able to communicate with the Westerners. Karma already had a working knowledge from speaking with his clients but their parents were too old to begin to learn a new language.

'Textbooks,' she told Karma. 'English textbooks and tapes are what we need.'

The two youngsters seized every opportunity to speak English, borrowing some textbooks from another nomad family and studying every night. They would often work together until two or three o'clock in the morning, up to the point when their fingers were so frozen they could no longer turn the pages.

During the day Tashi would look for chances to chat with the Western climbers. Her natural confidence soon won her a bunch of friends and she learned the words which were vital for the family's new job.

Knot, barrel, tent, blanket, string, rope, jacket, hat, boots, sleeping bag ...

She wrote all the vocabulary down in a small notepad and kept it with her constantly so she could slip it out and practise.

Then, in the tent one evening, their father made a proud announcement.

'We've got our first job,' he said.

They had to report at 5 a.m. the next morning, to the tents belonging to a Czech expedition.

This was their big chance, Tashi knew, and they had to get it right. She was so excited, she could hardly sleep that night.

She could not know that death would haunt their first trip up the glacier.

CHAPTER 6

When they arrived at the Czech camp, Tashi thought there had been a mistake. The pile of gear was so high it looked like the expedition was off to war.

'We'll never get all that on the yaks,' she told Karma.

'There's no choice,' Karma said grimly. 'That's the job.'

Tashi was astonished at how much weight the poor yaks were forced to carry. The expedition had tons of gear and wanted to pay for as few animals as possible. Two forty-kilogram barrels was standard, one loaded on each side of the beast.

Then other things would be laden on top. Tables, camera tripods, stoves, all the gear that couldn't fit into the barrels.

The creatures grunted and groaned as the weight was added to their backs. They were intelligent enough to understand that more kilos meant more pain. Tashi could see their legs shaking with the strain.

'It's too much,' Tashi complained. 'It's no wonder so many of them go lame.'

'They have to earn their living,' her father told her sharply. 'Just like us.'

The loads were dangerous for the yaks but the rate of pay for the family was excellent, each day giving them the equivalent of what they could earn in a week anywhere else on the plateau.

'We're going to be rich!' Karma said.

Tashi put her fingers to her lips. She was more superstitious than her brother and didn't like to tempt fate.

They set off, their father walking the first few kilometres alongside them.

On that first journey Karma showed Tashi the route to Advance Base Camp, a demanding trek of twenty-five kilometres along two different glacier systems. The journey was never entirely safe; the slopes above the pathways were unstable and prone to sudden rockfall. The clattering thud-thud-thud of cascading boulders was a constant hazard.

On Tashi's very first journey a yak belonging to another family was killed in front of her eyes. A huge boulder came down from above, caught the creature broadside, hurling it into a deep crevasse. The young boy in charge of the yak escaped by the skin of his teeth, leaping to one side at the last moment.

'Are you OK?' Tashi and Karma hobbled their own animals and ran to his aid.

The boy nodded and the young Tibetans stepped cautiously to the edge of the crevasse. Deep in the bowels of the glacier they could see a hint of dark fur, hear the lowing of the dying beast.

Then the creature fell silent.

Later Tashi heard that two Western climbers had abseiled down into the crevasse to retrieve the climbing equipment. The yak was sealed for ever in that frozen tomb.

Every night on the glacier was an adventure, pitching their tent in the midst of the wildest possible conditions. Karma didn't seem to have learned all the tricks of camping, Tashi began to realise – probably because he had always slept in tents put up by expeditions he was working for – and they made some early mistakes which cost them sleepless nights.

On one occasion they pitched the tent far too close to one of the fast-flowing channels of meltwater that run like veins across the surface of the glaciers. At three o'clock in the morning they had to move in a hurry when they discovered the banks of the channel had eroded towards them. In just a few hours the route of the raging torrent had shifted almost ten metres.

'We could have drowned tonight,' Tashi told Karma.

If the tent had fallen into the channel it would have been the end of them.

One night there was a sudden storm. Tashi and Karma were alone and they hadn't secured the tent very well. The glacier ice was too hard to penetrate with pegs so they had tied the guy ropes to small stones and left it at that.

It wasn't enough. The wind sprang up suddenly in the early hours and whipped the anchors out in seconds. Tashi and Karma woke with the flapping of the canvas as the tent threatened to blow away into the night. Freezing sleet beat against them as they stumbled out to try and pin it back down.

Within seconds they were soaked to the skin. Then Karma dropped and broke their only torch. A guy rope lashed against Tashi's face, catching her painfully in the eye. Their three yaks had broken free of their ties. Now they were panicked by the storm's lightning, lumbering this way and that, dark shapes with glittering, fearful eyes.

'We have to catch them!' Tashi had yelled at Karma. 'Find some rope!'

A lethal chase kicked off, running to and fro across the slippery surface of the glacier as the storm raged. The yaks were in a dangerous mood, kicking out when Tashi or her brother got close. Two of the animals had a full head of horns and at one point Karma was almost gored in the belly.

It took a very long time to pacify the yaks and bring the exhausted animals back to a safe spot where they could be tied.

The storm took another three hours to blow itself out. Tashi and Karma huddled together to share their body warmth, wrapped in the remains of their tent. Tashi had never been so cold. By the time a grey sheen of light crept across the dawn sky she could hardly feel her hands and feet.

'We'll have to go back,' Karma said. 'The yaks will get sick if we keep going to the camp at the col.'

'We finish the job,' Tashi said firmly. 'If we don't get these barrels to the camp we won't get paid.'

Twenty-four hours later they arrived at the foot of the North Col, children and animals utterly exhausted. Tashi knew she had taken a risk to push the yaks so hard but she reasoned she had only done what her father would have instructed her to do.

They were paid three hundred dollars for the load carry and a fifty-dollar note each as a tip. Things had worked out. But only just. Tashi knew that she and Karma could not afford to mess up again.

Every decision up here was a potential matter of life or death.

△

By the middle of June all of the serious climbing expeditions were gone and the summer trekking groups began.

The monsoon clouds would gather every day, laden with tropical moisture from the Indian Ocean. The yaks had lighter loads and the days were warm, even though snow often fell.

When there was no carrying to be done, Tashi sometimes got work helping out in other ways. She would prepare food for the trekkers, put up endless rows of tents, use a foot pump to blow up the inflatable mattresses; anything to earn some extra cash.

'Winter will be on us before we know it,' her father often reminded her. 'We need savings to survive.'

Tashi got other interesting opportunities with the trekking groups. Opportunities to go high.

Six thousand five hundred metres had been her previous

altitude record. But now, having got friendly with some of the leaders, she was invited to climb with the teams on their most challenging days.

She carried the medical kit, or a couple of tanks of oxygen in case of a medical emergency.

The climbs were on 'trekking peaks', Himalayan mountains which were non-technical but high enough to be serious.

Seven thousand metres. Seven thousand three hundred.

Tashi got used to wearing crampons clipped to her boots, the sharpened steel spikes giving her the freedom to move where she wanted.

'I'll teach you how to use an ice axe,' one of the leaders promised her after a trek.

Tashi spent a couple of exciting days learning ice-axe techniques on the glacier. She got a taste for it, and began to wonder if one day she might get an opportunity to go even higher.

The frosts began in September, the ground freezing as hard as iron. A disturbing rumour started to spread amongst the yak herders, news of an atrocity in which Tibetan pilgrims had been fired on by Chinese troops as they crossed the Nangpa La, a well-known trekking route into Nepal.

Several Tibetans had been shot, Tashi heard, and one nun killed. It was disturbing to think of such things happening so close to Base Camp.

The authorities denied it had ever happened.

Work dried up. The bitter temperatures kept tourists and expeditions away. Many of the yak drivers moved their animals down to lower altitudes, quitting Base Camp with little regret.

'Why don't we follow them?' Karma asked. 'Give the yaks a break and us as well.'

'We stay here,' their mother said. 'We can't afford to travel.'

They all knew the real reason why. Travelling would mean checkpoints, the danger that their forged identity cards might be challenged.

Winter seemed to last for ever. Tashi ached for longer days and warmer times. Her previous home on the plateau had been a full thousand metres lower, in a comparatively mellow zone of Tibet, blessed by long hours of sunlight and mild winds.

By the end of March the grasslands where she grew up would be alive with spring flowers and the sounds of crickets and birds. Rivers ran free. Animals emerged cautiously from their long period of sleep and hibernation.

At Everest Base Camp winter just went on. And on. Even at the end of April the rivers could be totally frozen, not a flower or bird to be seen.

In this deep-freeze environment finding nutritious food for the yaks was a constant battle. They needed plenty of fodder to sustain them on the long treks and there was virtually no useful grazing at such extreme altitude.

Hundreds of sacks of grass and hay were transported up to Base Camp in trucks. The price was extortionate but the yak herders were forced to pay. The only other choice was the starvation of their animals.

Human food was also brought in by road. Not even barley would grow properly at the altitude of Base Camp. Tomatoes and onions came in from the lower regions of Tibet. Fruit was shipped up from Nepal. Everything was costly, at least twice the price of the same produce in nearby towns.

Again there was no choice. It was pay. Or starve.

Tashi was glad when the expedition season came round again. There were lots of familiar faces, and many of the leaders asked for the services of Tashi and Karma.

Sometimes the expeditions just wanted their barrels of equipment to be shifted as fast as possible up to Advance Base Camp.

They paid a bonus for a quick delivery.

Tashi and Karma had plenty of energy. Occasionally they did a five-day round trip up the glacier with fully laden yaks then returned to Base Camp for a couple of hours to load up again and set off straight away for another job.

It was a punishing routine; one that many of the older men couldn't match. They needed a few days' rest between journeys, liked the comfort of their warm tents and their glasses of rice wine after the freezing nights on the glacier.

Tashi and Karma quickly became known as the hardest working yak drivers at Base Camp.

△

Dealing with the international members of the expeditions was an almost daily event. There was interaction when the yaks were loaded, the coming and going as blue barrels and kit bags were weighed and tied tightly in place on the backs of the animals.

Then there were the long treks up to Advance Base Camp.

The foreigners were open and friendly with Tashi and her English quickly improved. Goading the heavily laden yaks up the glacier was hard work but it was common for the expeditioners to walk alongside the yak chains and Tashi was good at making friends. She loved it when the climbers chatted about their home lives, their families back in Australia, America or Spain.

'Tell me about your country,' she would ask. 'Are there mountains? What animals do you keep?'

In this way Tashi learned much about the world.

One day an American climber showed Tashi some holiday photographs of his children. They were standing in front of the pyramids of Giza in Egypt.

It seemed incredible to Tashi that children had such opportunities. Flying halfway round the world to experience the wonders of an ancient civilisation. It was unthinkable that a Tibetan child would own a passport and even a Tibetan adult would have to wait years with no guarantee of getting one.

Sometimes the foreigners would make throwaway comments about inviting her to their homes.

'One day they will take you to America,' her father said.

Tashi laughed. Her father's remark seemed utterly crazy. And yet it fired a thought in the young Tibetan girl.

Were the climbers serious about their invitations? Could she somehow get hold of a passport? Fly in an airplane? See the places that the climbers had described to her?

It was an impossible dream. Besides, Tashi knew she could never leave her family. What if her father got even sicker than he already was? Or one of their animals died?

Fate had been kind to them since arriving at Everest. But that could quickly change.

One thing never failed to amaze Tashi: the amount of photographs the foreigners took. Dozens every day. She was always happy to smile for their shots and secretly she longed for a chance to take a few photographs herself. Cameras fascinated her.

Then, one day, a Polish woman climber handed Tashi her Canon to take a portrait posing in front of Everest. Holding the camera in her hand was a revelation to Tashi. It felt so *right*.

The plastic body was so perfectly shaped to her hand. The way her fingers curled around the moulded shape felt like the object had been designed for her and her alone. Raising the viewfinder to her eye came as naturally as breathing. The tiny screen seemed like a window into another world.

'Smile please!' Tashi pressed the shutter release.

The exposure time was one thousandth of a second but that blink of a mechanical eye was enough to give Tashi the desire for more. Much more.

Tashi worked for the same Polish lady six weeks later, hauling her tents and equipment back to Base Camp.

The woman was in a jubilant mood after a successful expedition and she wanted to share her joy with Tashi.

'Tell me about summit day,' Tashi begged.

'I can't remember much,' the climber told her with a smile. 'Just a mixture of tiredness and pain. It was worth it though for the view. Just incredible!'

Tashi tried to imagine how special it would be to see the Himalaya from the highest point on earth. All her life she had loved to be amongst mountains. They chatted for hours as they descended the glacier.

At Base Camp Tashi got a surprise.

'I want you to have this,' the Polish lady told her. 'I can see how much you love to take photos.'

She handed Tashi her Canon digital SLR.

Tashi was astounded. Her heart thumped wildly in her chest. She turned the camera in her hands, not quite sure what to do or say. Then she made to hand it back.

'It is too much,' she said shyly. 'But thank you anyway.'

But the climber was insistent.

'I have two other cameras,' she said with a smile. 'And I want this one to be a souvenir of our happy times on the glacier.'

She embraced Tashi warmly and insisted she accept the gift.

From that moment there was rarely a time when Tashi did not have the camera close to hand. There was no instruction manual but the Polish climber had left her with a small solar-powered battery charger and a couple of spare memory cards.

Tashi got plenty of help with her new hobby. There were usually two or three keen photographers amongst every team and sometimes she even got a chance to show her pictures to a professional. She took every opportunity to learn, and every opportunity to shoot.

In six months she mastered the complicated functions of the camera, building a stunning collection of photographs which documented the life of the Everest yak herders in wonderful detail.

Then something unexpected happened. The editor of an American wilderness magazine came out on an Everest trek and got talking with Tashi. As soon as he saw her portfolio of photographs he made a surprising offer.

'I want to publish these,' he told her. 'I can put them in the August edition.'

The article was titled; 'Shooting on the Roof of the World' and it used seven of Tashi's best shots. The text described Tashi's life.

Tashi was sent a single copy of the magazine and it

became one of her most treasured possessions. It was locked in the family strongbox in the tent and kept in pristine condition. Whenever she felt in need of a boost Tashi would bring out the magazine and stare in wonder at the images. It was magical to see her pictures in print and she yearned to do more.

Tashi was paid fifteen hundred dollars for the spread; everything in her world was going so well.

She should have known that it was all too good to be true.

△

One day a convoy of army jeeps pulled in to Base Camp. Tashi was tending to the yaks on a rare day off so she witnessed the arrival of the very last person on the planet that she wanted to see.

Chen.

Tashi ducked down behind one of the yaks as he climbed from his vehicle. She was close enough to see the scowl of displeasure on his face as he looked around the organised shambles that is Base Camp.

'This place is a stinking mess,' he snapped to his subordinate. 'Get these Tibetans to take their yaks further away from the camping area.'

'What's he doing here?' Tashi asked a friend.

'Haven't you heard? He's the new Base Camp commander.'

Tashi ran to the family and told them the news.

There was a stunned silence for a few moments then Karma sprang up and drove his fist hard against the wooden pole in the centre of the tent.

'I hate him!' he cried. 'We're happy here. Why can't he leave us alone?'

'We mustn't panic!' their father urged. 'He doesn't know we're here. Not yet at least.'

Karma sank down on to the cushions, his head in his hands.

'I'm not going to go on the run again,' he told the family. 'I had a year away from you and it was the worst time of my life.'

Tashi reached for her brother's hand.

'Karma's right,' Tashi's mother said emotionally. 'From now on we stick together, whatever happens.'

The family went quiet. Tashi looked to the small shrine which sat in the corner of the tent. Had their gods abandoned them, she wondered?

'I should do some sort of protest,' Karma said. 'There's plenty of journalists around here who'd be interested in my story.'

Tashi felt a familiar spasm of fear. She had always had a hollow feeling that her brother's impulsive streak might lead him into even greater trouble.

'That's not so smart,' their father said. 'It'll just inflame the situation.'

'Or maybe Chen just won't find out I'm here,' Karma said. 'There's hundreds of us yak herders after all.'

'There are spies everywhere,' their mother reminded him. 'Once Chen finds out we are here it will only be a matter of time before he gets you.'

'There's only one option left to us,' their father announced.

The family sat in silence. No one wanted to say the word.

Tashi bit her lip. The thought of leaving Tibet was almost unbearable. Just when things had started working out so well at Base Camp.

'We'll have to sell the yaks and whatever else we can. Bribe our way across the border. Make our way to India.'

Tashi swallowed hard. A sharp stone seemed to have lodged itself in her throat.

'I can't think about this now,' Karma said quietly.

Karma packed a sleeping bag and some survival rations into a small rucksack and went to hide out in one of the hermitage caves high on the valley wall.

Tashi left the tent and watched her brother go. Then she turned towards Everest, the mountain that had brought the family so much prosperity and peace. The holy mountain had saved them once. Could it save them again?

Or was exile the only answer?

△

A rumour started going around. Word amongst the yak herders had it that Chen was at Base Camp because he was being punished by Beijing for a serious misdemeanour; that it was a way of teaching him a lesson.

The incident on the Nangpa La began to be linked with his name. The one that Tashi had heard about, where the Tibetan nun had been killed by Chinese troops as she went on pilgrimage.

Was it Chen that ordered his soldiers to open fire on those pilgrims? Was that why he was now wearing the uniform of a lowly recruit? Why his three shiny stars had vanished?

The incident had been reported all round the world, a blatant example of brutality on the part of the Chinese towards the local Tibetan population.

Certainly Chen looked to be in a poisonous mood as he stomped around his new domain, poking his nose into everything in an intrusive fashion. The previous Base

Camp commander had been a kindly type who just got on with his job and went no further.

Chen, on the other hand, looked like a man who was spoiling for a fight. He seemed to particularly despise the yak herders, announcing that he would start a programme of random searches for contraband or banned religious items. He was drinking heavily too. A crate of cheap Indian liquor was delivered to his tent every few days.

Tashi was working with a Swiss team at that time. The leader, Christophe, told her that, back home in Geneva, he worked for a charity that campaigned for religious freedom in Tibet.

Tashi told him about the Tiananmen Square incident and it piqued Christophe's interest in the new Base Camp commander.

'I've got a satellite internet feed into my tent,' Christophe told her quietly. 'There's some sites I can check out for you. Try and find out more about this guy.'

Tashi was treading on eggshells, hiding herself away, terrified that Chen would recognise her. Her father was secretly trying to sell the yaks, but things were going slower than he had hoped and he had had no offers. If he couldn't sell them there would be no journey into exile. Neither of the parents was well enough to survive a trek across the Himalaya on the rugged smugglers' trails.

They would need to cross one of the border points which were known to be manned by corrupt officials, something which was only possible with hefty bribes.

Tashi took to wearing her ski goggles and face scarf around Base Camp, particularly when she knew Chen was around.

A couple of days after their conversation, Christophe pulled Tashi aside.

'I've got more background on our "friend",' he said. 'There are websites that chart the dark deeds of Chinese officials and his Tiananmen stuff is on there.'

'Yes? What did you learn?'

'Chen was a star recruit,' Christophe told her. 'He graduated top from Beijing's most prestigious officers academy. It seemed he was headed right for the highest echelons of the army, perhaps even destined to become a general.'

Tashi frowned, thinking about the empty bottles stacked outside his tent.

'So how come he ended up like he is?'

'That protestor he shot,' Christophe said. 'He was the son of a high-ranking politician, a member of the politburo. It was a terrible irony; the politician was one of the people who sat in an office and ordered the army to slaughter their own people. Inadvertently he caused the murder of his own son.'

'But Chen couldn't have known that, could he?' Tashi said in a shocked whisper. 'He was just following orders, yes?'

'Yes,' Christophe agreed. 'But it cast a shadow over his entire career. He was sidelined to Tibet where he's been getting more and more bitter and twisted ever since.'

Five more days passed. Tashi continued to hide herself, skulking round Base Camp without being noticed by Chen. Then there was a meeting of the yak herders to discuss the compensation rates for animals that were lost on the glacier. Tashi was there, not expecting that the Base Camp commander would attend.

When Chen swept into the tent the meeting became stilted; the Tibetans were reluctant to speak out in front of the boss. Tashi hid her face as best she could.

Chen suddenly pointed at Tashi.

'Take off that stupid mask,' he ordered. 'You look like a bandit.'

Her hands trembling, Tashi did as she was asked.

Chen went rigid.

'I know you,' he barked. 'Come outside.'

Tashi's guts turned to ice. She followed the Base Camp commander out on to the moraine.

'I haven't forgotten you and your family ... ' he said with a thin smile. 'How is your brother, the criminal?'

Tashi held her head high and looked him right in the eye.

'He's not a criminal,' she said.

Chen's attention was drawn to the camera hanging from Tashi's neck.

'Let me see that,' he said.

Tashi passed it to him. Chen turned it in his hands.

'This is worth thousands of dollars,' he said. 'How did you get it?'

'It was a gift from a climber,' Tashi replied, well aware how unlikely it sounded.

'A *gift*?' Chen exclaimed. 'My goodness you must have done something quite extraordinary to earn it.'

'It was a lady from Poland,' Tashi said. 'We were friends. She wanted to encourage me … with my hobby.'

Chen stared hard at her, his dark eyes not flinching. Then he stepped closer, his voice lowering to a whisper.

'I'm going to go back through the records,' he said. 'Look in the books and see if any climbers have reported a camera lost or stolen in the last few years. Then we'll see about your "gift".'

He handed the camera back to Tashi.

'Now. Are your parents here?'

Tashi nodded.

'Come on then.'

△

Tashi led the commander to the tent. Her parents went pale as they saw the imposing figure enter.

'Greetings!' Chen said. 'A pleasure to meet old friends.'

And so the interrogation began.

How long had the family been at Base Camp? Had they heard from Karma recently? Had they seen him? Did he still engage in criminal activities? Was he still a devotee of that counter-revolutionary the Dalai Lama? Was he plotting against the government of Beijing? Was he planning to incite further riots?

'We have nothing to tell you,' Tashi's father replied to each and every question.

Chen steadily became enraged.

'You play an innocent game,' he said. 'But let's see if there is evidence to the contrary shall we?'

Chen began to rummage through the family's meagre possessions.

Tashi felt her throat clamp up as she saw his fat fingers running over her personal things.

Then he found Tashi's special magazine. The one featuring her photographs.

'What is this?' Chen asked.

He thumbed through the pages, then stopped, scowling,

as he found her article.

'It's you!' he exclaimed.

'Yes! The editor came here and saw my photographs.' Tashi whispered. 'He wanted to use them.'

'A foreigner asked you to take these?'

'No. The photos were my idea, sir,' Tashi felt her heart spinning. She clenched her fists together behind her back. She wanted to leap at Chen, snatch the precious magazine from his hands.

Chen looked at the inside page, tutting when he saw the details of the publisher.

'An *American* magazine,' Chen said suspiciously. 'You are working for the Americans, taking photographs in a sensitive border zone.'

Chen ripped the magazine in two and tossed the halves to one of his guards.

He continued his search and, underneath Tashi's sleeping mat, he found a book. He took a look at the title then held it between two fingers, at arm's length, like it was a piece of stinking dirt. It was Tashi's copy of the Dalai Lama's autobiography, *My Land and My People*.

'This book is forbidden,' Chen said. 'It is illegal.'

'It shouldn't be,' Tashi replied. 'It should be read by everyone who wants to know the truth.'

'Oh yes? And what does your wise guru say on *that* subject?'

'Our freedom has gone,' Tashi said. 'Our land has been stolen from us.'

'He doesn't mention that this was a lawless wilderness of savages until we came?' Chen said quietly. 'A place of bandits and murderers, devil worshippers and warlords? Without schools and roads and industry apart from stealing each other's animals! Did he say that? Did he?'

'No,' Tashi replied. 'Why would he say that when it's not true?'

'You've left me no choice,' the commander said gravely. 'I will have to report your counter-revolutionary activities to the authorities, see what action they want me to take.'

He handed the Dalai Lama's book to one of his men.

'This is evidence,' he said. 'Guard it well.'

The man nodded, holding the book like it was a hand grenade or some other lethal weapon.

'Don't even think about trying to abscond,' Chen said. 'I will have my guards watching this family day and night.'

'We'll look forward to that,' Tashi's mother said bitterly.

'Meanwhile I will make more enquiries about your son,' Chen said. 'See if anyone has seen him here at Base Camp.'

Chen and his men left the tent.

CHAPTER 7

Tashi ate with her parents that night but no one had much appetite. Even her favourite barley soup tasted sour on her tongue.

'Why do we put up with this?' her mother spat. 'It's not his business to interfere. He's here to see the expeditions run smoothly, not persecute us. We should tell the others and get a demonstration going to get him removed from the post.'

'He's been appointed by Beijing,' Tashi's father said. 'If we protest they'll send the army in like before.'

The family went quiet as footsteps marched past. Chen had been good to his word about keeping them under watch. Soldiers were passing close by the tent every half an hour.

'Do you think someone will tell him Karma has been

working here?' Tashi asked.

The family went quiet. Tashi saw her mother and father exchange a quick glance with each other.

'None of the yak herders will say a thing to Chen,' her father said. 'But there are others who might not be so loyal.'

Tashi got no sleep that night. She couldn't stop thinking about her brother, alone and freezing up there in a desolate cave.

Later, other moments from Chen's visit played in her mind: confiscating her copy of the Dalai Lama's book. Ripping up her magazine.

Tashi knew she could soon get another copy of the book, but the article might not be so easy. The magazine had been a talisman. Something to be proud of. Something that was hers, born from her passion for photography. It was a symbol of her independence, her potential to become something more.

In the darkest hours of the night Tashi swore something to herself: Chen wouldn't get his hands on her camera.

First thing in the morning Tashi took the camera to the man that ran the Base Camp store. He placed it in his strongbox for the time being, away from Chen's prying eyes.

Several days went past. Tashi felt continuously nauseous and jumpy. Her father had still had no offers for their animals.

Chen took to walking past their tent several times a day. Was he getting a kick out of provoking them? To Tashi that seemed the most likely thing. The man was a sadist, dangling them on a string.

Tashi made clandestine journeys up to the caves every evening, taking Karma food and tea. Her brother was out of sorts with the world, bored and restless.

'Chen's been asking around for information about you,' Tashi told him. 'But there's a pact amongst the herders. No one's telling him anything.'

Karma began to make occasional trips down to the camp, making sure to keep away from Chen. He was taking crazy risks but none of the family could tell him to stop.

At night he retreated back to the caves, curling up tight through the long, freezing nights.

Another day went by. Then came a breakthrough: an offer was made for the yaks. The deal would be concluded in five days when the purchaser had the cash.

'We'll leave for the border as soon as we have the money in our hands,' Tashi's father told her.

Tashi waited for nightfall and went to relay the news to Karma.

'You've only got four more nights in hiding,' she told her brother. 'I'll do one more journey to Advance Base Camp and that will be it.'

Karma nodded. He understood the reasons for Tashi to keep working. If the family suddenly stopped taking the expedition loads, questions would be asked by Chen.

'Hey, I've got a great idea!' Karma exclaimed. 'Why don't I come with you? There's no guards up there and Chen would never think we'd have the nerve. It will give us one last trip together on Everest before we go.'

Tashi thought about it. Karma's proposal was outrageous but she loved the idea of being up there with her brother a final time before their journey to exile began.

'We'll do it,' she agreed excitedly. 'Meet me in the morning two hours out of the camp, where the glaciers join.'

△

Tashi loaded her yaks with the Swiss expedition's equipment the following day. Christophe and his team were a jovial bunch, experienced climbers who had ganged together to pay for an Everest permit. Some of them were very young, university students who liked a joke.

Tashi felt her cares lifting as she started the journey up the glacier. She beamed with pleasure as she saw Karma trek down the valley side to join them.

Karma also got on well with Christophe and the leader

was interested to know more about the children's 'crimes' of owning a portrait of the Dalai Lama and a copy of his autobiography.

'It's a violation of human rights,' he told them. 'You should be free to express your religious convictions.'

'Human rights don't mean anything here,' Karma told him. 'The authorities do what they believe is correct and they don't care what any other country thinks.'

The conversation was fascinating to Tashi. The idea of a charter of human rights was one that she had never thought about before. The more Christophe told them about it the more she wondered how on earth the Chinese could get away with their treatment of the Tibetans.

'The West is too frightened to offend Beijing,' Christophe explained. 'They don't want to lose their markets in the East.'

Tashi felt anger burning deep inside. The people of Tibet had a right to be treated fairly but that right was being ignored by the whole world. It seemed totally wrong.

The trek came to an end all too soon. The yaks were relieved of their burdens and it was time to begin the journey back down.

'Can I ask a favour before we go?' Karma said. 'Tashi's told me about the Tiananmen Square demonstrations but

I've never seen any of the video clips. Could you show me?'

'Sure,' Christophe agreed.

As soon as the mess tent was erected, he fired up his laptop and got online.

△

For almost an hour, Karma and Tashi watched the video footage from Tiananmen Square. Christophe knew a great deal about the atrocity and was able to add a lot of detail.

Karma was horrified by what he was seeing, but also amazed by the scale of the demonstrations.

'A million people,' he said in wonder. 'Just imagine a million people all believing the same.'

Karma could hardly bear to watch the footage of the young Chen shooting the unarmed protestor. He put his hands over his eyes, shuddering with disbelief.

Then Christophe asked, 'Have you heard of Tank Man?'

'Tank Man?'

'Let me find him.'

Christophe entered the words 'Tank Man' into the search box and a new video clip came up.

Tashi and Karma saw military tanks rolling into the square. The display of force was chilling. The demonstrators were largely gone but a hard core of protestors still remained.

Then the camera zoomed in. Picked up a column of tanks as they rumbled forward.

'Look at the man!' Karma suddenly gasped.

A civilian had walked over briskly to the leading tank and placed himself defiantly in its path.

Tashi gasped at the raw drama of the moment. For a second she feared that a soldier would simply pop up from the tank and shoot the man dead. He seemed just an ordinary type, a businessman or trader.

The tank swerved. The civilian adjusted his position. The tank dodged in a different direction. The man did the same.

'Cat and mouse,' Christophe said. 'With everything at stake.'

The clip ended.

'What happened next?' Tashi said. 'Did the tank roll over him?'

'The person filming had to stop. No one really knows what happened next or if that man survived.'

He turned off the laptop. Tashi stared at the blank screen, her mind buzzing with thoughts.

At that moment footsteps approached the tent. It was one of the yak herders, red in the face and exhausted.

'I've just run up the glacier,' he panted. 'I've got bad news.'

They gave the man a seat and he caught his breath for a moment before continuing.

'Chen found out you've been at Base Camp,' he told Karma. 'He knows you're up here and he's got a dozen soldiers coming to join him. He says he's going to arrest you in the next twenty-four hours.'

△

Karma got to his feet, began to pace up and down the tent.

'I'm trapped,' he said grimly. 'It's over.'

'Information is power,' Christophe said reassuringly. 'At least you have the advantage of *knowing* that they're on to you.'

'He's right,' Tashi agreed. 'We're still one step ahead of them.'

'This is a huge valley,' the leader continued. 'There are hundreds of places you could hide for a couple of days.'

Karma shook his head angrily.

'What if I don't want to keep hiding?' he said. 'What if I don't want to keep running? This is my country, isn't it? What right does Chen have to persecute me?'

Tashi felt her stomach churn. The anger was growing inside her brother. Was this news that he was about to be arrested going to tip Karma over the edge? Could he even harm himself? Tashi forced the thought out of her mind. Karma was a bit hot-headed sometimes but she felt sure he wouldn't put the family through the pain that such an action would bring.

'I'm going for a walk,' Karma said. 'Try to get my mind clear.'

Tashi and the expedition leader stayed in the tent, talking through the situation as they waited for Karma to return.

'I worry he's going to do something extreme,' Tashi said. 'He's been getting more radical as he gets older.'

'He's under a lot of pressure,' Christophe agreed. 'But that's the story across the whole of Tibet. Young people beginning to say enough is enough. Look at all the young monks that have burned themselves in protest, dozens of them, some of them just in their teens.'

Tashi trembled as her blood chilled. The thought was too much to contemplate.

When Karma came back into the tent, Tashi saw to her surprise that her brother somehow looked different. A lot of the tension in his face had gone and he seemed calm and confident. The Swiss leader gave him a steaming cup of hot chocolate.

'I've made a decision,' Karma told them. Tashi could see the fire in his eyes.

'Yes? A decision to do what?'

Tashi felt her heart beat faster.

'I want you to take me with you,' he said to Christophe. 'Let me climb and do a protest on the mountain.'

Tashi thought the Swiss guy would laugh in Karma's face. But he didn't. He just nodded and said,

'OK ... you took me by surprise there but I'm open to anything. Tell me what you're thinking.'

'I want to take my flag, my Tibetan flag, on to Everest,' he said. 'Get a photo of it on the summit if I can. Get publicity in newspapers, television. Tell my story.'

'*What*?' Tashi stared at her brother. 'You have to be joking, right?'

'No. No joke. I mean it.'

'But ... but you've never been climbing before,' Tashi said. 'How will you survive up there?'

'You know the truth is, it's really not so complicated,' Christophe said with a small laugh. 'The skills are basic.'

'You remember Drugi last year?' Karma added.

Tashi nodded. Drugi was a young yak herder just like them. He had been offered a job as a high-altitude porter by an expedition and to everyone's surprise had got well above eight thousand metres with hardly any training at all. If he hadn't twisted his ankle he might even have reached the summit.

'It's largely about fitness,' Christophe said. 'And you guys are doing the perfect training, every single day.'

Tashi could see his point. Trekking up and down the glacier was an ideal physical preparation for climbing.

'As for the equipment, we've got lots of spare clothing and gear. We can lend you what you need,' Christophe added.

Karma nodded his thanks.

'It was those videos,' Karma said. 'Think about all the people in that square, how brave they were.'

Tashi shivered as she remembered the man standing in front of that tank.

'You're right,' she conceded. 'I feel different as well.'

'We have to be like them,' Karma said. 'Make a stand. Swallow our fear and not run away.'

Tashi felt a raw buzz of love for her brother. His courage was inspiring. And frightening.

'I should discuss this with my team,' Christophe said. He left them in the mess tent and went to consult with his expedition.

Ten minutes later he came back with two of the other climbers. They went straight to Karma and embraced him warmly with words of welcome.

'OK,' Christophe said. 'We're totally up for this. We'll employ you as a high-altitude porter. Fifty bucks a day.'

Karma's face split into a huge grin.

'You'll have to pull your weight,' he warned. 'Carry a load every day like the rest of us, yes?'

'Of course!' Karma beamed. 'I will carry as many kilos as you like!'

'When it comes to your protest we'll also help in any way we can, take photos and video for you, but you understand later we may have to tell the authorities we didn't know what you were planning?'

Karma nodded.

'I get it,' he said.

'Maybe we can get into a bit of trouble,' Christophe said with a wry smile. 'But to be honest we're on your side and we'll take the risk.'

'Can we start tomorrow?' Karma asked eagerly.

Christophe looked to his climbing buddies. They nodded, smiling.

'Sure,' he confirmed. 'We were planning to start our climb first thing tomorrow anyway. So when your Captain Chen and his soldiers arrive you'll already be out of reach.'

Demons flocked into Tashi's dreams that night. She woke up in a cold sweat at dawn, fearing that Karma might have left without saying goodbye. But her brother was sleeping next to her, his breathing calm, his hair covered with a glistening sheen of frost.

Tashi watched him for a while as the steely grey light of daybreak slowly lit the tent. *Karma*. She smiled as warm memories flooded back. The endless jokes he played on his friends. The things he had done to help or protect his big sister over the years of their childhood. He was no longer a child, she realised. His decision to climb Everest marked the end of that phase of his life. It was an unbearably sad thought.

After breakfast Tashi prepared the yaks for the journey down the glacier. Karma watched her work, standing outside the Swiss mess tent, his expression still fixed and calm although there was a hollow depth to his eyes which spoke of deeper doubts.

'What will you tell Chen?' Karma asked. 'You're going to bump into him today as you head down.'

'I'll tell him you ran away. Vanished last night. He won't get any more out of me, I promise.'

Karma nodded.

'What am I going to tell Mother and Father?' Tashi asked.

'Tell them the truth,' he replied. 'I hope they will respect me for what I am doing.'

Tashi smiled. She stepped forward and hugged her brother close.

'Just come back alive,' she said. 'That's all that counts.'

Karma nodded, then turned away to join the others.

CHAPTER 8

Tashi's story was finished and as if to underscore the drama of her tale, the ground shuddered with yet another aftershock. The earthquake wasn't finished. Not yet.

We grabbed hold of the poles of our improvised shelter, helping it stay upright while we waited for the shaking to subside.

'Now you understand why my brother is up on Everest,' she whispered.

I certainly did. And much, much more. The story of how her family had been blocked from their ancestral lands, the herd stolen from them by unfeeling officials, had left me sickened.

Klaus had warned me about the human rights abuses

on the plateau of Tibet, but I hadn't expected to actually meet someone whose life had been turned upside down by such injustice.

I took Tashi's hand. Her fingers were ridiculously cold.

'Do you think my brother could still be alive?' she asked.

I thought about the rock avalanche I had seen sweeping down the face after the first massive quake. The chances of anyone surviving seemed small, but I didn't want to kill all hope for Tashi.

'He might be,' I said. 'Anything is possible. Why don't we go back to the Swiss tent and try again for information?'

'Ok,' Tashi said. 'Let's do that.'

We picked our way through the hazard zone that just a few hours earlier had been a fully functioning Base Camp and found the Swiss tent once again. This time there was a member of the Swiss team – a shell-shocked looking radio operator – but he had little to offer in the way of encouragement.

'I know your brother,' he said sadly. 'But we cannot be optimistic for him. I've been on the radio for hours trying to reach the high camps but there's no reply.'

'There must be survivors,' Tashi said. 'Maybe he's one of the lucky ones.'

The radio operator shook his head sadly. 'I understand

how you feel,' he said. 'But no one can help your brother now.'

'Please can you try it again?' she begged.

The man put in a final call, holding the headphones to Tashi's ear so she could verify it for herself.

Static. Nothing but static.

'I'm sorry,' the man said.

'How about getting a helicopter up there?' I said. 'See if there are any signs of life?'

The man shook his head emphatically.

'No helicopter can fly so high. The air's too thin for the rotors to get lift.'

He put his head in his hands.

'I'm up to my neck in this nightmare,' he sobbed. 'Your brother's not the only one who's been killed. What can I say to the relatives? I have to call them now ... '

We walked away from the Swiss tent and found a boulder to sit on. A thin cloud of wood smoke had drifted across from some nearby tents and was now suspended in the air. The silvery blue smoke was like a veil, drawn across the scene. I was struck by how peaceful everything looked now it was dark. The violence of the earthquake seemed like a cruel trick of the imagination.

Had it really happened? The falling rocks? The avalanche

of iron-hard ice? The deaths and injuries? I longed to wake from this nightmare and find it was all a dream. For Tashi to wake tomorrow to see her beloved brother Karma striding back down the glacier.

We turned to the mountain, scanning the moonlit slopes, feeling the familiar emotions of awe and respect that Everest commanded. Was there still a chance? Could there still be a few survivors in the high camps?

It was true that the rescue team had reported no remaining tents, and avalanche debris several metres deep.

'There must be places people could hide,' Tashi said. 'Caves. Overhangs. Places where a climber might crawl for safety?'

I let my mind dwell on some of the more troubling scenarios. Her brother could be injured, unable to call for help. I shivered. It was too distressing to think about.

The cold was beginning to bite. Tashi pulled her duvet jacket tight around her shoulders, her breath creating glittering clouds of icy vapour. We knew we should be heading back to the tent, but neither of us could tear our eyes away from the mountain.

Then we saw it.

A flicker.

A light.

A brief and brilliant pulse. Exactly at the site of Camp 6. The place where Karma was last seen. It came again. I heard Tashi's breath quicken.

'Someone *is* up there,' she said. 'Someone's alive.'

'Yes. I saw it too. Definitely a light.'

'It could be Karma,' Tashi said excitedly. 'It could be him!'

△

We watched for another half an hour, until our eyeballs were virtually freezing in their sockets. But there was no more flash.

Then came a siren blast and a voice called out by megaphone:

'Meeting now at the Base Camp commander's tent. Meeting now.'

Within ten minutes every single climber was gathered together, waiting expectantly for news. It was almost exactly eight hours since the earthquake had struck and the mood of the assembled teams was a potent mix of raw grief coupled with shock.

In total there were almost five hundred people, roughly divided into three categories: Western climbers, their Sherpa high-altitude porters, and the local Tibetan yak drivers like Tashi.

Finally the boss arrived. Chen. A megaphone in his hand. I felt my fingers curl as I saw him. I knew now what misery he had inflicted on Tashi and her family.

He clambered on to the remains of an old cairn to give himself some height, switching on his megaphone and adjusting the volume as it howled back noisily.

'I have had instructions from Beijing,' he pronounced. 'Everest is closed for this season. There's likely to be aftershocks, more danger. It's over for this year.'

There was a stunned silence for a few seconds. Then the babble of conversation from all sides.

'Transport will be arranged back to the Nepal border,' he continued. 'You have forty-eight hours to strip the mountain and leave.'

'Is there any further news about fatalities at Camp 6?' someone asked.

'My team have inspected the mountain,' Chen replied. 'There's no one left alive up there and the area is too unstable to allow anyone else in. You can take down remaining tents from the lower camps in the next two days, but Camp 6 is out of bounds.'

A clamour of voices erupted, all desperate to be heard.

'We saw a light!' Tashi called. 'A flash coming from Camp 6. Less than one hour ago.'

'One at a time!' Chen snapped.

He didn't hear Tashi's call.

'What about our permits?' one of the leaders yelled. 'Will they still be valid for next year?'

'It is too early to say,' Chen replied. 'Beijing will make an announcement on this very soon.'

The response caused a ripple of consternation. Each of the climbers had paid more than ten thousand dollars for the permit to climb and I guessed many of them would struggle to afford the fee again.

'Don't you think this is an overreaction?' another climber protested. 'If you had a democratic vote now with a show of hands you'd find that most of the climbers here want to carry on.'

A buzz of agreement rippled through the crowd.

'That is irrelevant,' Chen replied. 'The mountain is closed and that is final.'

The meeting broke up, the teams dispersing to spread the news to sponsors and loved ones back home. We ran into an expedition leader from an international team, a New Zealander I had walked with for a few hours on the trek up the glacier.

'Come back to the mess tent,' he offered. 'Have a hot drink and warm your hands on our heater.'

We joined the team in their hastily repaired mess tent. Everyone was exhausted and dirty, the mood grim. The international team hadn't lost any members in the avalanche but they had lost friends. We both accepted a mug of steaming tea and the leader got the portable heater going for us to cluster around.

'You sure about that light?' one of the climbers asked.

'Yes,' I replied. 'We both saw it.'

'Who do you think it might be? Have you got a friend up there?'

'My brother Karma,' Tashi replied. 'It's his first time to go high on the mountain. He's carrying the Tibetan flag with him, hoping to get a picture holding it at the summit.'

'Respect for that,' one of the expeditioners commented. 'Sounds like his heart's in the right place.'

'He's a good person,' Tashi continued. 'But now I'm not sure he will be coming home.'

A deep silence kicked in. No one knew what to say.

'If he missed the rockfall, how long is it possible to survive up there?' Tashi asked.

'I heard about an American woman who survived eight days buried in an avalanche in the Rockies,' one of the climbers said.

'People can live for ten days at the highest camps if

they've got enough oxygen,' said another.

'But the Chinese have made a search,' Tashi said. 'They say they can't find anyone alive.'

'Pah!' the expedition leader exclaimed, 'they just want to close the mountain with a minimum of fuss. Do you really think they've searched every cave, every overhang, every crevice where a climber could hide from the earthquake?'

'I don't know … '

'One of my friends came down from the high camp just now,' a Sherpa chipped in. 'He told me he never even saw a search team up there.'

'It's a long shot,' a German climber said. 'But your brother could still be alive.'

As the conversation played out I was watching a magical transformation take place. Tashi had entered the tent in a state of despair. Even the flashing light had begun to seem like a figment of our imagination. But now there was a different spark in her eyes; the spark of possibility. There was even a bounce to her step as we left the tent.

We went back to our shelter, filling the pan with blocks of ice so we could melt more water in the night. It was mind-blowingly cold, perhaps twenty or thirty degrees below freezing. A stubborn layer of cloud was blanketing the whole of Base Camp, reducing visibility to a matter of metres.

Zombie-like figures occasionally shuffled out of the gloom, climbers searching for personal belongings that had been blown far and wide over the glacier.

The distant crackle of unseen walkie-talkies buzzed. Climbers were still on their expedition networks, talking to their Sherpa support, arranging for their higher camps to be dismantled and brought down the mountain.

Tashi went to some Tibetan porters that were sheltering in the wreckage of a nearby tent and begged some juniper wood. We roamed the glacier until we found a puja cairn which was still upright and she then burned the fragrant wood whilst chanting prayers. I prayed as well, in my own way, wishing that I could understand the local language.

Tashi stared at the mountain for a while. Her face was serene, totally calm. But her expression was also ruthlessly determined.

'I'm going up to find my brother,' she said. 'Permit or no permit, I'm going up.'

I stared at her for long seconds. Her eyes were unblinking and filled with confidence. I already felt I knew her well enough to know she wouldn't joke about this.

'Do you want to come with me?' she said. 'I'll be leaving first thing in the morning.'

△

My first reaction was no.

Of course I can't come and climb Everest.

I haven't got any gear. Haven't had any training. My name doesn't feature on any official permit. Oh, and I'm scared half to death of the mountain!

Is that enough? I asked myself. Or do I need a few more reasons?

'I understand,' Tashi assured me. 'It's not your problem after all.'

Her words cut into me. The rescue of her brother certainly *should* be my problem. Tashi had helped save Klaus's life so I certainly owed her one. And I had seen that flash up at Camp 6 just as clearly as she had.

Was it cowardice?

Night fell. We watched the blue gas flame burning as the wind teased the exterior of our small shelter. I couldn't resist finding out more about Tashi's plans.

'How long will you be up there?'

'I don't know. I guess two or three days to get to Camp 6, then I'll have to see what happens.'

'Where will you get the gear from, the oxygen and so on?'

'I think those guys from the international team will lend me what I need.'

I thought about my friend Kami, wondering what he would advise me to do in this situation. I reached into the side pocket of my rucksack and retrieved the shrine bell.

The shrine bell. It felt so good to hold it in my hands, to remember the sacred trust that had been placed in me to become its guardian. I felt the carved wooden handle, always warm to the touch. I pressed it gently to my nose, smelling the sweet scent of incense – sandalwood and jasmine – that had been absorbed over countless ceremonies, countless rituals.

The bronze of the bell was touched with golden light from my head torch. The metal was scuffed, burnished by use over tens of years. It felt to me like it was infused with magic and prayers and the positivity of faith. I thought about how close this precious artefact had been to the summit – just a few tens of metres. Heartbreakingly close. How devastated Kami had been once that mission had failed.

Then the strange twists of fate that had shifted the responsibility to me. The request from the heart, from Kami's girlfriend Shreeya, to one day finish the task. To get the shrine bell to the summit, to complete the quest.

Could I do it? I truly had no idea.

I packed the precious bell away and checked out the cooker. The pan of ice had melted down and it was time to drink.

As the small hours of the night dragged past my mind turned full circle. Thinking about Kami and the shrine bell had shifted my point of view. Was I crazy? An opportunity to get myself on to Everest for real had come up and I was dithering about it. What was wrong with me?

I began mulling over the permit situation, wondering if there was a way to duck the system. Under normal circumstances I knew it would have been impossible; the Chinese control over foreigners' movements would never have allowed it. There were too many safeguards to make sure individuals couldn't break free from the groups. The guides watched over everyone with an eagle eye. But our guide had evacuated to Lhasa with Klaus and the situation at Base Camp was one of total chaos. Hundreds of climbers were moving out; yak herders were working twenty-four hours a day, portering all the gear down the glacier.

The lower slopes of the mountain would be busy. Climbers would be rushing up and down to retrieve their gear from the lower camps. It was obvious none of the normal systems were functioning; the liaison officers had lost control.

Most of the soldiers had been called away to help clear landslides from the roads. The remaining guards were occupied full-time on other tasks to restore order after the avalanche. If I went off the radar for a week who would really notice? If ever there was a good moment to disappear in Tibet this was it. No one would even know I had vanished.

The crashing noise of distant rockfall woke us early the next day. The grey light of dawn was just filtering into the shelter.

'I dreamed about Karma,' Tashi said. 'Dreamed he was alive, stuck in a cave.'

Tashi fired up the gas cooker and went out to replenish the ice bags as I laid out crackers, cheese and jam. The two of us forced down as much food as we could.

'I'm coming with you,' I told her.

Tashi's smile was radiant. She threw her arms around me and gave me a big hug.

'Of course you are,' she said. 'I knew it. Now let's go and get the gear and see if we can rescue my brother.'

△

Tashi's instinct was correct: once he understood our crazy mission the expedition leader from the international team had no hesitation in offering us the loan of ice axes, crampons and other hardware. He had spare wind suits, helmets and plastic boots as well.

'We'll be back next year anyway,' he said. 'So you can

just leave them at the store place near the monastery when you're done.'

His offer of assistance went further.

'We've got a stash of six oxygen bottles above the North Col,' he told us. 'We were going to go up and retrieve them but if you want to use the O^2 we'll just "forget" about them.'

He drew us a small diagram to show where the bottles were situated beneath a marked cairn on the ridge.

'You should practise putting on the gear,' the leader suggested. 'You have to get the basic things right.'

The leader took us over to a quiet corner of the glacier and, for the next hour, we went through the routines of putting on the climbing gear over and over again. Tashi had done it all before but for me it was a vital session. I found fitting the crampons to my boots was the trickiest part. I repeated the process many times until I was confident I could get it right every time.

'Now some jumar training,' the leader told us.

He set up a short length of rope, showing us how to snap our jumar clamps on to it, practising the technique of moving up a fixed line.

'It's basically all easy stuff,' he observed. 'But you really have to know it.'

Tashi smiled proudly at me when we were done.

The session had boosted our confidence, but I could sense her growing impatience.

'We need to move fast now' Tashi said. She pointed to the sheer wall of intimidating ice that sat behind the camp. 'The North Col is waiting.'

I scanned the rampart, noticing the deep crevasses that split the face. I knew from my reading that seven Sherpa climbers had been swept away and killed in an avalanche in that very place on one of the early British expeditions and it made me shiver to think of the risks.

At the top of the col was a huge overhanging cornice, a hanging glacier that looked precarious and poised to fall.

'What do you think?' she asked.

'Scary.'

'We'll take two litre bottles of water each.' Tashi advised. It was already shaping up to be a warm day by Everest standards.

One hour later we began our trek through the camp, a sprawling area many hundreds of metres across.

'We don't want to get too close to people if we can help it,' Tashi said.

The two of us weaved a route through the area, bypassing the tents as best we could. We were relieved to see that our presence attracted no attention; there were plenty of other climbers heading up towards the col that morning to retrieve their gear.

We fitted in fine.

I felt more confident with every step but I knew we could be challenged at any point. The earthquake had caused widespread chaos but there were still Chinese liaison officers around.

These were the people to avoid, I knew. A random permit inspection could cause the whole plan to collapse.

'That's Chen's tent,' Tashi muttered. We skirted round it, keeping our ski goggles on tight, pulling our face masks up high as if we were protecting ourselves from the sun.

We passed through the final tents and hit a rocky plain. The sun had crested the high ridge above us. A shimmering haze of heat was beginning to radiate off the dark rocks. From a distance it had looked like a five-minute walk to get across this area but forty minutes of hard walking got us halfway across with the temperature rising fast.

Conversation petered out as we climbed the rising slope. The thin air was already giving me a nagging headache but I didn't want to admit it to Tashi when we'd only just begun. I knew that acclimatisation was going to be a problem for me; I hadn't been at altitude for long enough for my blood to fully adapt. My red blood cell count would be high, but nowhere near as high as Tashi's. It was one more thing to worry about.

'Need to lose some layers,' Tashi said. I agreed with her. I could feel trickles of sweat running down my spine. We stopped, taking off our outer Gore-Tex layers and drinking cool water from the bottles.

Half an hour of further slogging through the heat brought us to the base of the ice cliff. There were four or five climbers there, preparing to go up and fetch down gear. They said hi but didn't try to talk further.

We shrugged off the rucksacks and pulled our equipment out. We helped each other to fit the gear, stepping into the harnesses and snapping the metal frames of the crampon spikes to our plastic boots.

'Double the loops through the buckles.' Tashi reminded me quietly. 'Every detail helps to keep us alive.'

I was proud of how well we put on the kit. The test runs had given us vital practice and we certainly hadn't looked incompetent or suspiciously slow.

We clipped our jumar clamps on to the line and began to move up. I couldn't stop a huge smile running across my face as I realised I was truly on Everest. The big E! Climbing. Moving up the fixed lines.

What would my Nepalese friends Kami and Shreeya say

if they could see me now? If they knew I had their sacred shrine bell with me, safe in my jacket pocket? It was an amazing feeling. I was on Kami's mountain.

For real.

△

'Not so fast,' Tashi protested after fifteen minutes of quick progress. 'You won't keep that pace going.'

I realised she was right. Raw enthusiasm had led me to move too quickly. I was puffing and panting hard in the thin air.

I learned to move slower, swinging each leg up and kicking the front points of my crampons gently into the ice. Kicking too hard was another beginner's mistake, I realised. All it achieved was bruised toes and a load of wasted energy.

Climbing the col was intensely thrilling but it was a bizarre feeling to look up the slope. The teetering towers of ice above us were so still, so quiet, it was hard to believe they could kill. They looked almost beautiful, sculpted by the wind into soaring columns, twisted by the glacial pull of gravity into fantastic shapes reminiscent of cathedral spires. It was tempting to think of them as benign, I thought, a photo opportunity, or merely something to be appreciated for its wild beauty and locked away in the memory.

Then came a crack. The sound of splintering ice. A shuddering of the face beneath our feet.

'Watch out!' Tashi screamed.

A series of blocks came tumbling down the slope, spinning fast towards the valley floor. They weren't too big, just chunks really, but it was a sign of how unstable the hanging glaciers of the col could be. A shimmering cascade of ice powder hissed past us.

I picked up a piece of the debris that had come to rest nearby. It was only the size of a watermelon but it felt heavy and dangerous in my hand.

'Feel that!' I tossed the chunk to Tashi.

'Wow!' Tashi tested the weight of it. 'I'm glad we've got the helmets.'

The helmets, yes, I thought. But no helmet in the world could protect us from one of those ice towers if the whole thing gave way. It would be like being buried beneath a collapsed apartment block.

'The gods are looking down,' Tashi said, 'they will protect us.'

I smiled. I was learning about Tashi's faith: always there, giving her strength in every situation and I wished I felt the same.

From time to time, strange sounds came from deep

beneath the face.

Halfway up the ice cliff I felt a pressure headache kicking in. The altitude was beginning to bite.

'I need to rest,' I told Tashi.

I flopped down on the snow, my body pulling at the safety line as I turned to see how much height we had gained.

The camp was now pleasingly far below our position, dozens of expeditions laid out across the valley floor on the widest part of the glacier. Most of them were packing up after the closure announcement and I felt a pang of regret as I saw the long line of climbers trekking down towards the Rongbuk monastery. Those climbers could have helped us, could have given us backup, but they were all going home. It reminded me of just how crazy our rescue attempt really was.

We were moving away from safety, on an illegal expedition. With no support. On a mountain that would soon be deserted. It was an intimidating thought, and not for the first time I wondered if the whole mission was utter madness. There were a thousand ways we could fail.

Then I thought of what this rescue meant to Tashi, and I felt my determination return. I couldn't let her down, not now I understood the deep reasons for Karma's Everest climb. We would just have to try our best.

CHAPTER 9

'Let's drink,' Tashi said. We passed the flask of warm tea between us, letting our bodies recover a bit.

While we rested, a Japanese climber wearing a massive rucksack came down the ropes and plopped down next to us. He looked worn out, and happily accepted Tashi's offer of a sip of tea.

We sat for a while, looking out over the valley, enjoying the majestic sweep of the East Rongbuk glacier as it snaked away towards Base Camp.

'You guys going up to clear a camp?' he asked.

'Uh-huh,' I nodded, hoping he wouldn't question why we were going UP with such big packs.

'Which team are you with?'

I felt Tashi's eyes lock on to me in a silent warning.

'We're on a shared permit,' I told him. 'It's an international team.'

This was the cover story we had agreed on. 'Shared permit' teams were often just loose collectives of climbers with no real leader. Keep it vague was our plan.

The man nodded. 'Did you lose anyone in the earthquake?'

'No,' I replied. 'We were lucky.'

The climber scrutinised us closely for a few seconds.

'You're both pretty young aren't you? How old are you?'

'Loads of people have said that,' Tashi said nervously. 'Let's just say we're a bit older than we look.'

The comment hung in the air as the Japanese guy considered it. He stared at Tashi, obviously waiting for her to say more. Tashi blushed red but kept her mouth shut. The Japanese climber shrugged.

'OK. Well good luck anyway!'

He clipped on to the line and started to descend.

'We should cover up more,' Tashi said. 'If he noticed how young we are, then everyone will.'

'You're right,' I agreed.

We joined the fixed line once more, gaining a further two hundred vertical metres over the course of the next couple of hours. The climbing was tough work, but that wasn't the only challenge now we were on the real flanks of Everest; the reflected sunlight off the face was brutal. Both of us were burned on the cheeks and nose before we realised it.

'We need to get the glacier cream on earlier,' Tashi observed.

In our eagerness to leave we had simply forgotten to put on the protection. Now we took out the tube of cream and slathered it on to every inch of exposed flesh.

The last three rope lengths to the col led us on to the steepest ice yet; it wasn't far off vertical. I used the front points of my crampons, thrusting the ice axe in as deep as it would go. The ice anchors wobbled alarmingly. Touching them revealed how insecure they really were. I doubted they would hold the weight of a real fall. It felt like they would rip right out with the least provocation.

It was a massive relief to reach the lip of the col. I hauled myself up the final section of fixed rope with weary determination, clipping myself off the line as I reached flat terrain. I sat down heavily, taking in the view that now opened up.

The North Col was narrower than I had expected, a ridge of ice about three hundred metres long and, in some places, as little as ten metres wide. Fissures and crevasses meant that there were only a few areas where tents could be put safely.

From below we hadn't been able to see much. Now we saw that there were still a few clusters of tents dotted along the ridgeline, colourful splashes of yellow and red domes set against the brilliant white of the background ice. Climbers, mostly Sherpas, were dismantling the tents and packing up gear. The evacuation was well under way.

We rested, drinking a little tea from our flasks, then trekked along the ice ridge, weaving through the disassembled camps and searching for a hidden spot to pitch our tent.

'It's like a war zone,' Tashi commented.

Many of the climbers were exhausted, lying outside their tents. Some were bandaged up, returning with minor wounds from high camps after the earthquake. Others were tending their stoves as they prepared tea before heading off down the col.

'How about here?' I said. I had found a small area behind an ice ridge. It was just big enough to take a tent.

'Let's do it.'

We would be nicely out of view.

△

Using our ice axes, we scraped out a flat surface. The ice was as hard as rock and the task took twice as long as I had expected. We were sweating hard by the time the platform was ready.

Then we erected the tent, threading the Kevlar poles that gave it shape and pinning it down with every single peg at our disposal.

'Not bad!' I was proud of what we had done. The tent looked solid.

'Let's eat before it gets dark,' Tashi said. She gathered a plastic bag of ice to melt.

I set up the cooking stove and spun a spark out of a lighter. The gas ignited with a satisfying hiss. I found a packet of pasta in my pack. Packets of tomato soup came from the depths of Tashi's rucksack, along with a cooking pan and a hard piece of Tibetan cheese.

When the water was boiling, we added the soup powder and threw in the pasta at the same time.

'The wind has dropped away,' Tashi said, 'we can eat outside.'

We left the tent, finding the col pretty much empty. Almost all of the teams were now retreating down the fixed lines towards base.

'We're just about the only ones here,' Tashi said.

It was a lonely feeling.

We put down our foam mats and ate the food in the most spectacular place imaginable, perched on the very edge of the North Col, looking directly down on to the camp some six hundred metres below.

'I keep thinking about Karma,' Tashi said. 'It feels wrong stopping like this.'

'We're going as fast as we can,' I reassured her.

Tashi nodded. She knew as well as I did how dangerous it would be to keep climbing without night stops. Altitude sickness would stop us dead in our tracks long before we got to where Karma might be found.

We turned to look at the vast North face of Everest, tracking the sinuous line of the ridge then following the gullies and rock walls up ... and up ... into the rarefied heights of the summit pyramid where a billowing veil of snow crystals scudded into the late afternoon sky.

'He's being blasted by that wind,' Tashi said. 'They say it can be more than a hundred kilometres an hour at Camp 6.'

I tried to imagine the power of such a force, wondering how Karma could survive it. Had he found shelter? Would his equipment be enough to keep him warm? Would a tent survive even a single night of such an onslaught? I had no idea.

'Eat your food,' Tashi said. 'Before it freezes.'

I stared at the plate of pasta, surprised and disappointed to find that I didn't feel hungry at all. In fact the sight of the food made me feel a bit ill, another curious effect connected to the high altitude.

'Don't think about it,' Tashi advised as she saw me pushing the pasta about the plate. 'Treat it like fuel.'

We sat for a while, eating a little, then Tashi spotted activity down at Base Camp.

'There's another expedition arriving down there,' she said quietly.

I saw the movement she was talking about. A line of about twenty tiny figures was crawling painfully slowly up the glacier into the Base Camp zone.

'They look like soldiers,' Tashi said hesitantly. There was no mistaking the tremor in her voice. 'You can tell by the colour of their clothes.'

I felt the hairs rising on the back of my neck. It was true the team were wearing military khaki and were now gathering close to Chen's tent. Had the Base Camp commander somehow got wind of our illegal climb?

'You don't think they're going to come up after us do you?' Tashi said fearfully.

'I doubt it,' I replied. 'It's probably some sort of routine expedition.'

A glacial silence embraced us as vivid fears kicked in. My words had sounded hollow. The prospect that a military team was pursuing us was a true nightmare. The plan to rescue Karma had always relied on speed and surprise. And secrecy. Now it looked like we had a team of soldiers to contend with. And they were just one climbing day behind us.

We would have to move faster than ever.

△

I forced the food down, finding some comfort in the warmth it gave me. We went back to the tent and zipped up our sleeping bags. No conversation passed between us other than a brief good night. The sight of the army guys had freaked us both out.

I was dead tired but I lay awake for hours, thinking about how crazy this rescue mission really was. Was that military team really going to climb up after us? Would we arrive to Camp 6 to find Tashi's brother dead? A headache began to pulse in the back of my skull.

The wind started to howl at high altitude. Somewhere above us Everest's famous plume was beginning to run. The almost musical tone of it lulled me into an uneasy sleep.

Tashi was awake at dawn.

'Wake up!' she urged. She shook my shoulder until I

emerged, reluctantly, from the cosy embrace of my sleeping bag.

Tashi packed snow and ice into the cooking pot. The tent was soon filled with the reassuring roar of the propane cooker. We added instant porridge to the cups, along with several spoons of sugar and a handful of raisins. The oats were warm and filling, but I felt a dull pain in my throat every time I swallowed and my head was still throbbing like crazy.

'Think I need to take a couple of these,' I told Tashi.

I popped two paracetamols from their pack.

'It's the altitude,' she told me.

I swallowed the painkillers and we dressed in our mountain gear. Out on the col, a few Sherpas had just arrived from Camp 5. They must have climbed down in the night.

They greeted us with friendly calls as they trekked past to the top of the fixed ropes. Their loads were massive. Each of them had a rucksack twice the size of ours. One turned back.

'You guys know the mountain is closed, right?' he asked.

'Yes, sure,' Tashi replied.

'Just checking.'

He gave us a curious look, then turned and joined his friends.

'Let's pack up the tent and go,' Tashi said. 'The clock is ticking every moment.'

We hurriedly packed up the sleeping bags and cooking gear. Twenty minutes later, the tent securely folded away in our rucksacks, we stepped over a series of narrow crevasses which marked the edge of the col and made it to the first of the fixed ropes on the ridge.

Step. Slide the jumar clamp up the rope. Kick in. Repeat. Rest. Breathe. Suck the painfully thin air into hungry lungs. Repeat. Step. Slide the jumar clamp up the rope. Kick in. Repeat.

We stopped frequently, drawing in air and looking nervously back towards the col. Were the military team coming up? We desperately needed to know, but for the first couple of hours we simply couldn't tell; the angle of the ridge blocked the view. As we gained height, however, the perspective opened up.

'Oh no!' Tashi was the first to see them.

The mystery team was halfway to the col.

'They must have left really early,' Tashi said heavily. 'And they're moving fast.'

I nodded, trying to make a mental calculation of how many hours behind us they were.

Six? Eight? It was feeling too close for comfort.

'This is such a disaster,' Tashi said despondently. 'Even if we get up to the Camp 6 zone before they catch us, they'll get us on the way down.'

'Don't think about it,' I urged her. 'We just keep going as fast as we can and that's it.'

Tashi rummaged in the side pocket of her pack, pulling out a packet of dried apricots. The fruit was frozen solid but it hardly seemed to matter, the sweet tang of it on the tongue was enough to restore our spirits and give a vital spike of energy.

We clipped back on to the line and resumed the climb. I felt my pulse rate quickly rise as my body warmed to the activity.

For a while everything felt OK. Then the headache kicked in harder and I started to feel sick.

'You alright?' Tashi asked.

I bent over my ice axe. My legs were feeling as heavy as lead.

'Sure ... '

I didn't want to tell her how bad I was feeling.

The weather was changing too; the crystal blue skies of early morning had given way to ugly grey clouds. The sun had vanished in a sulk and a boisterous wind was playing along the ridgeline.

An hour went past. Tashi tapped my arm.

'Someone's lost a pack,' she said. 'Up ahead.'

I saw a tatty mess of colour on the slope.

'Maybe they dropped it,' I suggested.

We got closer. Something white was gleaming from the midst of the faded reds and yellows. I began to think it might not be a lost pack at all.

'Oh!' Tashi exclaimed. 'It's a body.'

△

My mind took a second or two to process her comment. Not until I was standing right over the corpse could I really see it for what it was. A fallen climber. His bones picked clean by ravens. The bleached white object we had seen was the man's skull.

The body really was like something out of a sick horror film. The mouth was gaping wide in a perpetual scream. The teeth were shattered. One arm was thrown up in a gesture of seeming despair. Or was it an attempt to summon help? The right leg was bent back beneath the body. The left leg, most disturbingly, seemed to be missing.

I felt bile rising in my throat. My head swam as a dizzy wave of horror engulfed me. What had happened to the soft tissues? The flesh? Had the ravens stripped these bones? Or had the body simply rotted away?

I retched up the apricots.

'Your lips are blue,' Tashi said. She put her arm around me.

'Yeah? Just a bit hypoxic ... I guess.'

Tashi muttered a prayer.

We turned away from the skeleton, aware that something had changed. The dead climber had seemed like a gatekeeper, I thought. A guardian of the Death Zone, the highest reaches of the mountain where the combined effects of altitude and freezing wind become so extreme.

We struggled up the next fixed rope. I began to see stars in front of my vision.

'Take a drink,' Tashi said. 'I think you're getting dehydrated.'

I took a swig of liquid from my bottle, the super-chilled orange soothing the pain in my throat.

'We're only halfway up the ridge,' Tashi remarked.

I looked up, my heart sinking as I realised she was right. There was still a punishing distance to go before we reached the rocky ground at the top end of the snow slope. Many, many rope lengths stretching up as far as the eye could see.

'How about the soldiers?' I asked.

We stared down at the ice cliff of the col. The army team were eating up the challenge, coming up to the last third of the climb.

'Looking as strong as ever,' Tashi said glumly.

A coughing fit overcame me. My lungs felt raw and overstressed. The lack of oxygen was really beginning to strike. I had always known I was pushing it with the acclimatisation. I coughed again, my ribs aching with the spasms. Now I was getting really scared. High-altitude sickness could be a killer.

I unclipped my waist strap and shrugged off the rucksack, grateful to be free of the weight. The straps had been biting into my flesh for many hours.

I crashed down on to my side, feeling like I would black out at any moment.

'How much longer until we can pitch the tent? Maybe an hour?' I mumbled.

Tashi gave me a sympathetic look. 'Looks more like two hours to me.'

'Oh.'

I shivered. Resting for a few minutes had allowed the sweat on my back to congeal into chilling crystals of ice. I flexed my toes in my boots, felt them horribly cold and stiff. Frostbite could strike at any moment, I knew.

Being able to spot the first sign of freezing fingers and toes was a crucial part of staying alive.

'I'm not sure I can keep going,' I said. 'I'm just not acclimatised enough.'

Tashi suddenly became animated. She took off her ruck-sack and clipped it to the line.

'That oxygen stash is not far above us,' she said. 'I'll fetch a bottle and we'll see if that helps.'

'OK,' I nodded. 'Great idea.'

She flashed me a quick smile and stepped up the slope. Her climb rate was fast compared to mine and she was soon high above me and going strong.

I stared out at the mountain view for a while then re-membered my magical talisman, the shrine bell in my pocket. I took the tiny bell out, thinking of my Nepalese friend Kami as I did so. This had been his lucky charm. His spiritual inspiration to punch through the pain barriers on his own Everest climb the previous year. Now I'd hit my own pain barrier. Could the shrine bell help me?

I turned the little object in my gloved hands, sensing the familiar flow of strange spiritual power I felt every time I held it. Did this gift really have magic qualities? Kami's girlfriend Shreeya had certainly thought so.

'It must go to the summit,' she had told me. 'That is

where it belongs.'

I fell into a hazy kind of daydream, sitting there at seven and a half thousand metres, thinking of how Kami had been paralysed in an avalanche, how his spirit had never been crushed. How he could still smile and joke, the joy of life still beating inside him as strong as ever.

I felt better just thinking of him.

△

Tashi arrived soon after, slumping down on to the ice next to me with a sigh of relief. I helped to free her from her load, and the two of us sat, side by side, staring at the jagged peaks clustered to the south. Then our eyes fell, inevitably, to the col. Still the soldiers came up the lines. Like robots. Never slowing. Just a handful of rope lengths from the lip of the ridge.

'OK,' Tashi said. She pulled an oxygen cylinder and mask from her pack. 'Let's get you sorted out.'

We screwed the air line on to the regulator valve. Air hissed as it zipped along the tube. I pressed the mask against my face and Tashi clipped the strap at the back of my head.

'Wow!' I grinned.

The O^2 had a powerful effect. I could feel the cool

oxygen entering my lungs, altering the chemistry of my body with immediate benefits.

'The nausea ... ' I said in wonder. 'I can feel it getting better already... '

Tashi grinned with pleasure. Her mad dash up the ridge had been a brilliant idea.

'Thank you,' I said. I hugged her close, the oxygen mask banging awkwardly against her cheek so we both laughed.

I picked up Tashi's rucksack and helped her into it. Then she returned the favour, the dead weight sending hot daggers of pain into my already blistered shoulders.

Tashi led the way.

The oxygen helped me to pick up my work rate, giving my weary legs a bit more power. I still felt stiff though, and seriously tired. Tashi just kept on going, never complaining at all, her rasping breaths coming in rhythmic bursts as she muttered a Tibetan mantra to keep her spirits up.

My lungs felt better after a while. And the coughing eased off.

One hour passed. Four or five rope lengths ticked off. I felt optimistic I could make it to the camp zone but the thing about the soldiers played constantly on my mind. It was the feeling of being hunted. We were prey. If they caught us what would happen?

Twenty steps. Rest. Twenty steps. Rest. I looked at the grey mass of dangerous-looking clouds that had arrived with the afternoon. Distant rolls of thunder were warning of greater turbulence to come.

By 5.30 p.m. even with the extra oxygen every step was feeling like a test, run by some sadistic examiner. The muscles in my chest throbbed with the effort of sucking in air.

I stopped, staring up at the North Face, towering imperiously above us. The sheer size of it, and its obvious complexity, sent me into a black depression. As for Camp 6, a further thousand metres above our position, there was no visible clue that it had ever even existed. It really did look like the whole thing had been swept away.

I pulled my fleece hat tight against my ears, shucked up the hood of my wind jacket to protect my neck.

We made it to the Camp 5 zone with just half an hour of daylight remaining.

'You think we can jam the tent into this space?' I asked Tashi. We were standing above a scrap of flat terrain that looked no bigger than a tea towel.

'Maybe,' Tashi said.

It really was an awful place to camp but there seemed to be no other choice.

We unpacked the tent and erected it on the tiny platform despite the fact we couldn't get a single tent peg into the rocky surface. I got Tashi to squirm inside to stop the dome blowing away as I roamed around the slopes looking for loose rocks.

Once we were both inside we lit the stove, warming our fingers and toes back to life as the gas and our body heat slowly raised the temperature almost to freezing point.

We cooked pasta and sauce and drank about a litre of tea each.

Just before going to sleep I went out to fill the bag with more ice. Standing by our tent I stared down at the col and saw that the army team were pitching their camp there.

'They made it to the col,' I told Tashi. 'More's the pity.'

'You don't think they could do a double day tomorrow do you?' Tashi wondered. 'They'd catch us as we arrive at Camp 6 if they can.'

I didn't reply. Nothing felt very certain any more.

CHAPTER 10

I was awake at 6 a.m.

I got the cooker going but as I searched for the teabags a vicious blast of wind hit the tent. The whole structure shuddered violently, as if swatted by a giant hand, twisting the Kevlar poles out of shape and almost flattening the dome.

Tashi woke, stirring groggily in time for a second devastating round of wind.

'Are we going to be blown away?' she asked fearfully.

All went quiet for a few seconds. Then came the whistling approach of another blast as it raced across the rocks towards us.

'The water!' Tashi warned. I snatched for the pan but the cooker had already overturned, sending the precious melted water spilling across the foyer. Yellow flames flared up as the gas ran out of control. I cursed, grabbed at the toppled stove, burning the tips of my fingers on the scalding metal as I turned it off.

'Hold on!' Tashi said. The two of us reached up for the roof, grabbing the fabric to stabilise it as the wind tried to rip us right off the face.

'I'll get more ice,' I said.

I jammed my feet into my plastic boots and laced them up. Even that simple action left me panting for breath. Tashi helped me into my down jacket and I pulled my fleece hat low over my ears.

I unzipped the front flaps, letting in a raging mini blizzard of swirling ice. The sudden exposure to the outside world was shocking and abrupt, the stone-hard crystals beating against my cheeks and lips.

'Quickly!' Tashi urged. 'We're filling up with snow.'

I quit the tent and stood up. The sudden rise from the horizontal gave me a dizzy moment or two as I squinted in astonishment at the fast-changing scene. The glorious mountain views were now gone.

Instead, the scene was filled with a terrifying primal power. A boiling mass of bruised clouds was churning up the sky to the south. Lightning strobed across the purple interior of the storm front, a muffled roar of thunder following a heartbeat later. The wind continued to play cat and mouse, easing off into a deceptive calm then springing back to life and clawing at the face with angry swipes.

I staggered backwards as a new front pummelled the face. It was like being body slammed in a rugby match.

Tashi shouted from inside the tent.

'You OK?'

'Yeah. But we're getting trashed!'

The wind had loosened all of the guylines tethering us to the rocky terrain. The ice blocks we had placed on the edges of the fabric had simply been blown away. The dome shape was sagging, the tent poles bent and twisted. And the storm was still gaining strength.

Suddenly the clouds parted. A momentary gap allowed me to see down on to the North Ridge many hundreds of metres below. Climbers were coming up! A line of eight figures were beating a determined trail up the ridge.

I felt my heart surge as a wave of dread engulfed me. The army men.

They must have left in the middle of the night.

△

It was a cunning plan on their part. Make a surprise arrival. Trap us as we sheltered in the tent.

The clouds swept back across, concealing the view. I waited for a few minutes but there was nothing more to see. I shivered, my body core already getting dangerously cold. I bustled into the tent.

'The army men are halfway up the ridge. We have to move!'

Tashi stared at me in dismay. A fresh blast of storm-force wind punched into the tent. I turned off the cooker. There was no time for tea now.

Tashi burst into action, rolling up her sleeping bag and stuffing it into the bottom of her rucksack. I did the same, packing up the stove and the cooking pans. No words passed between us as we stowed the gear away, but the shared sense of urgency was enough to see the task done in record time.

I kept my inner gloves on. I didn't want to check out my fingers just yet, even though they felt worryingly numb.

We wriggled into the wind suits, zipped up the hoods and pulled them tight against our heads. Then the plastic boots went on, followed by crampons and gaiters.

'What about the oxygen?' Tashi asked. 'Maybe I should use it as well today?'

'You'll be faster,' I agreed. 'Let's go for it.'

We connected Tashi's mask to one of the cylinders and placed the bottle in her rucksack. I helped her to put on the mask.

She unscrewed the valve, checking on the little circular gauge to make sure the oxygen was flowing.

'OK. I can feel it,' Tashi said.

We fixed my mask. I felt stronger as oxygen-rich air entered my lungs.

'Right. Let's go.'

I pulled my goggles down and went out first. Straight away I could feel that the wind had picked up speed, the storm now strong enough to make standing upright a real challenge. Tashi came next, reaching for my hand as she was blown sideways.

We stood by the side of the tent, huddled together for a few moments as the wind raged.

'This is crazy!' Tashi shouted. 'We're going to get blown off the face!'

A flurry of snow crystals swirled into us hard at that moment, as if in confirmation. We ducked down, protecting our faces from the needle impact of the ice crystals.

'Let's pack the tent,' I said urgently, 'We need to get moving.'

We brushed off the ice with difficulty.

'Hold it with both hands!' I told Tashi.

She grabbed at the tent, the stiff, frozen fabric flapping wildly as she tried to pack it away. For a few moments I feared the wind would rip it from her grasp but she managed to hang on to it, throwing it on to the ice and kneeling on it while she folded it up. Then we strapped it on to the top of my rucksack and Tashi took the poles.

I put on the pack. The weight was a shock and I figured there must be a few kilos of ice that were still encrusted on the fabric of the tent.

'I can see them!'

Tashi's warning cut through the rip of the wind.

I whipped around, seeing that the clouds had partly cleared below. There in the gully, the same gully we had just climbed, was the army team, coming up steadily. They looked strong. Horribly strong. Moving in a single line at a pace far faster than we had achieved.

'They're following our tracks,' Tashi said. 'Less than two hours behind us.'

'Duck down!' I warned. The followers had stopped. The leader raised his arm, pointing directly towards our position.

It was Chen. Although my vision was impaired by the

oxygen mask and goggles, I knew with a crushing certainty that it was him.

'They've seen us!' Tashi exclaimed.

Clouds returned to the face. The white-out resumed, hiding us from view, at least for the moment. I found myself in the bizarre position of actively wanting the storm to continue. The truth was that as soon as the clouds were swept away we would be perfectly visible to our pursuers.

'Let's climb!' Tashi said.

△

We set off up the ridge, following the tatty old ropes that acted as a guide.

One hour passed with no rest. Then another.

My throat was bone dry. A terrible thirst began to rage. Our emergency departure had put us in danger of dehydration.

Clouds were now embracing the peak. Visibility had dropped to some tens of metres and the wind had become a constant force. The howl of the gale had reached a new intensity, a deep sound that told of unimaginable power.

We left the ridge and began to move out across the face, still following the fixed lines. I had the sensation that a noose was tightening around our necks. The whole thing was spiralling out of control and I couldn't think of one idea which would enable us to shake off the captain and his men.

The ground became increasingly steep. The trail traversed beneath crumbling cliffs of fragile rock. Stonefall was frequent. We got used to the clattering sound of tumbling rocks.

'We're being bombed!' I called to Tashi.

Everest was falling apart.

A break in the clouds gave us a chance to see the Camp 6 zone for the first time.

Tashi gasped.

The avalanche had caused terrible devastation up here at the high camps. The entire face looked like it had been pulverised by missile fire, rocks fragmented, ropes swept away. The only evidence that humans had ever been here were small fragments of tent fabric and ripped-up sections of aluminium tent poles.

We stumbled across the face, horribly aware of the incredible exposure. A slip would undoubtedly lead to a fatal fall. Gradually we became separated, Tashi taking a higher route than me as we explored the debris.

Then she called out.

'Here!'

I made my way up the slope.

She had found a body, partly buried by rockfall. A hand was protruding through the stones, the fingers rigid and frozen hard. The side of a man's face was partly visible, a dark beard matted with ice.

'It's not Karma,' she said with relief.

I wondered what we should do. It seemed utterly wrong just to move away. Should we say a prayer over the body? Place some stones to make a grave?

Tashi reached out, her gloved hand taking mine and squeezing tight. I knew she felt the same way. Tashi muttered a Tibetan prayer. I couldn't understand the words but I could sense they were respectful and heartfelt.

We moved on.

Two more bodies came into view. One was a Sherpa, distressingly young, his face serenely peaceful in death. The other was a female climber, badly mangled by rockfall, golden hair twisted with frozen blood.

'Where is he?' Tashi said, her voice cracking with emotion. Then she called out: 'Karma!'

I shrugged off my rucksack and took out the flask. We shared the sweet tea, feeling our bodies energised by the sugar.

Ten minutes later we found yet another corpse. To our surprise he was dressed in military clothing.

'A soldier ... ' Tashi said. 'What would ... ?'

I noticed something glimmering in between two rocks.

I bent to pick it up, holding it gingerly.

A gun.

Tashi took it, turning it in her hand.

'Do you think ... ?' Her eyes locked on to mine, the darkest of all thoughts running through both our minds.

We stared up the slope. High above our position was a crack in the face.

'That looks like a cave,' Tashi said. A small tinge of hope had entered her voice.

Could this be it?

Tashi placed the pistol back on the ground.

We clambered up the slope, making a few awkward moves over the boulders. Tashi led the way, eager, pushing hard.

As the crack came into reach I realised it was more an overhang than a cave, but still a good sheltering spot. First came a ledge. We saw oxygen bottles stacked against a wall. Food packets scattered around. A cooker attached to a single gas canister. Then, pulling ourselves up higher, in the darkest recesses of the overhang we saw a shape. A figure in a sleeping bag.

A tousled head of hair shifted as the figure stirred. Two bright brown eyes opened wide in surprise as a sleepy-looking Tibetan face emerged from the protection of the down bag.

'Karma!' Tashi lunged forward, throwing her arms around her brother.

△

Karma pulled the oxygen mask away. A massive grin of pure joy stretched across his face.

'Come here, my sister,' he said. Tashi gave him a big hug and then pulled back so she could inspect him closer.

I studied Karma closely, struck by the strong family resemblance he had to Tashi. His face bore the same tell-tale marks of Everest that I had seen on the climbers back at Base Camp, the high points of his cheeks burned by altitude radiation, his eyes red with the same tiny haemorrhages that those guys had had.

Tashi pulled back the sleeping bag, drawing in her breath sharply as she saw the state of Karma's shoulder. He was wounded. The fleece he was wearing was holed, encrusted in dried blood. It looked a real mess.

'The avalanche?' Tashi asked hesitantly.

Karma shook his head. Tashi unzipped the fleece, pulling the fabric back so we could see an ugly circular wound punched right into the centre of his shoulder.

My mind flipped back to the gun.

'You've been shot.'

Karma nodded.

'Chen sent a soldier after me. He would have killed me if the earthquake hadn't happened at that moment.'

'Let me see,' Tashi said.

We helped Karma to sit up, a movement that caused him to cry out in pain.

'Turn a bit,' Tashi said. Karma twisted, and we could see the exit point of the bullet at the back of the shoulder.

'We have to clean the wound,' I said.

I rolled out my first aid kit, selecting iodine and cotton wool. I cut away the clothes from his shoulder and started to clear the dried blood away, realising that the sterile nature of this high altitude place was working in Karma's favour.

There was no infection. At least not so far.

'I thought there might be others coming after me,' Karma said as I worked on him. 'So I crawled in here to hide. That's how I got lucky, there was enough oxygen and cooking gas to keep me alive.'

'This is going to sting like crazy,' I told him. I squirted iodine right into the wound.

Karma clenched his hands into two tight fists but didn't cry out. He was incredibly courageous. I finished off the treatment by bandaging up the whole shoulder then safety-pinned the cut clothing back into place.

'We're going to get you down,' Tashi told her brother.

She unzipped the sleeping bag and we rolled Karma clear. I packed the bag up carefully and stashed it in my rucksack. His boots were lying nearby and we soon had him laced up and ready to stand.

It took several tries to get him to his feet. He was extremely weak and wobbly. We got him seated on a rock while we snapped his crampon spikes into place.

'When was the last time you ate?' Tashi asked him.

Karma shook his head.

'I've been melting ice,' he mumbled. 'Hardly any food, just a couple of tins of tuna.'

I poured him the remainder of my tea. Tashi gave him a hi-energy bar and he wolfed it down enthusiastically. Then he ate a Twix and another energy bar. The food and drink had a miraculous effect. Straight away Karma seemed more focussed and alert.

My mind snapped back to the immediate predicament. We'd been so busy sorting out Karma that we had almost forgotten about the troops coming up.

I walked forward and used a big boulder for cover so I could spy down on to the gully below.

Chen and his men were still a good couple of hours below our position. Their movement had slowed, the altitude had knocked their pace right back. One or two of the men were clearly suffering, dragging their feet and resting over their ice axes with their heads down for long periods.

Chen looked strong. In fact he was ranting at the men although they were too far away for me to hear his screams.

Wind flurries began to whip across the rocks. A huge bank of turbulent cloud was seething to the south. I shivered violently; the air temperature was dropping fast.

Tashi came to my side.

'We mustn't tell Karma the troops are coming up,' she said. 'I'm not sure his mind can cope with that right now.'

'OK,' I agreed.

Then I saw it: a second gully, heading down. It looked a bit steeper than the one Chen and his men were ascending, but it definitely led down to the fixed ropes near to the lower camp.

A new thought kicked off in my mind: could we use the storm to our advantage? Bypass Chen and his men in the white-out and skirt round them in the blizzard? Buy ourselves some time to get off the mountain while they searched for us on the higher slopes?

I told Tashi the idea. She looked at the steepness of

the second gully and reacted with just one word.

'Risky.'

'Correct,' I agreed. 'But we don't have many other options.'

Tashi nodded, her expression grim.

'OK,' she said. 'Let's try it.'

△

We returned to Karma and helped him to fix his oxygen mask snugly to his face.

'OK?' I asked him.

'Yeah, I'm fine.' The Tibetan boy nodded gamely but I could see his eyes were screwed up with pain behind the glass of his ski goggles. The wind was still intermittently ripping through the air at gale force, causing us all to duck instinctively every time a big blast came through.

Tashi adjusted the gauge on his air tank.

'Can you feel the oxygen coming through?' Tashi asked.

Karma gave a thumbs up.

'We'd better get going,' Tashi said.

I led the way across the face, stepping over the scattered debris from the earthquake. Karma walked stiffly after his long days in the shelter but he seemed to gain strength as his body got used to moving again. The cloud had now rolled in. Visibility was down to ten, sometimes only five metres, masking us completely from Chen and his team. That was the good news. The bad news was the danger of losing our way completely.

At the top of the gully I checked my watch. Almost 3 p.m. We had no more than four hours of light left. Speed was as vital now as it had been on the way up, perhaps even more so.

We began the descent, plunging through thigh-deep snow, and straight away got lucky. An old fixed line was dangling down the slope. It was buried in loose spindrift but a few sharp tugs were enough to free it.

'Lifeline!' Tashi exclaimed.

It was. Literally. Karma could abseil down the fixed rope. And it would prevent us losing our way down the gully.

We clipped Karma's harness on to a sling, attaching a figure of eight descendeur so that he could step safely backwards down the slope. He did a few practice steps and nodded with satisfaction.

'It's OK,' he said. 'I can do it.'

Karma used his good arm to steady himself. His bad arm was tucked inside his jacket.

We got stuck into it, Tashi and me using the fixed line as a handrail and helping to support Karma when he stumbled. The blizzard was intrusive, stone-hard ice granules smashing into us at high speed. The cloud got thicker and darker, to the point where it felt like night was falling. Fresh snow was cascading all around us. I began to think about avalanches. Thousands of tons of snow was surely gathering on the slope above.

At one point we thought we heard voices off to our left. Then came a shout, frighteningly near.

'Chen?' Tashi mouthed.

I nodded. It had to be. We were level with the soldiers, some hundred metres away from them through the raging storm.

'It's the army men isn't it?' Karma's voice quavered with fear.

'Don't worry about them,' Tashi said confidently. 'So long as the storm keeps up they won't find us.'

'We're resting too long,' I interjected. 'Let's get going.'

Tashi got up, showing no signs of the fatigue that she had to be experiencing. My respect for her was growing with every hour of this adventure. She was an awesome person. So much strength and self-belief. So much unquestioning love for her brother.

Together we pulled Karma upright, trying to favour his uninjured left side. I could see him flinch with the pain but he didn't cry out. Then we resumed the descent, stepping down on to the shiny layer of ice, our legs crashing awkwardly through the crust. I took the lead, breaking the trail, trying to ignore the painful impact on my shins.

I kept in front for an hour, then Tashi called:

'My turn.'

She shifted around me, letting me take position next to Karma. My knees started to play up, the constant jarring descent sending jolts up my legs.

The storm intensified, the wind was gusting fast enough that it threatened to blow us off our feet. On occasions we had to huddle together, clutching each other for dear life as the howling wind raced across the slope. The clouds seemed to suck all of the light out of the day and I felt my mood darkening just as fast.

I was beginning to become despondent. It was 5 p.m. and we were still struggling down the gully. Chen and his men would be arriving at the Camp 6 zone about now, I reckoned. Everything now depended on two factors: keeping Karma on his feet, and the cloaking effect of the storm.

What if Chen had guessed our trick?

I gave myself a mental slap. I had no right to be blue. It was Karma who had been shot and left to die at extreme altitude and he showed no signs of depression at all.

Compared to him I was fortunate. I knew I had to pull myself together.

'We can't stop at any of the camps,' Tashi said. 'We have to keep going through the night, all the way down the col.'

△

Darkness fell. We came out of the gully, on to the broader space of the ridge. Out of the protection of that narrow couloir, we were now subjected to the full force of the north wind.

We kept on down, clipping from line to line with our slings, not wanting to risk a single second without the protection of the rope. We used the head torches sparingly, just a quick blast of light when changing from one rope to another. The gusts became irresistibly strong. Twice I was bowled over, hitting the ice hard before scrambling back up. Tashi placed herself upwind of her brother, protecting him as best she could.

The fixed lines were arching into the night. Tashi just kept going. On and on – the strength of the girl was incredible. Karma was flagging though. Once or twice he stumbled forward. Tashi kept catching him, ever vigilant and fast to react.

At some undetermined point of the night I had an out

of body experience, the fatigue so extreme that I began to hallucinate. I saw myself from above, going through that endless process: place the ice axe, step down, place the ice axe, step down, over and over again. My movements resembled the juddery progress of an old man, I noted critically from my unreal vantage point, every limb stiff and spidery.

Then a blast of wind acted as a wake-up call. I came round, regaining awareness of where I was and what I was doing.

Karma could no longer hide his pain. Every step down caused him to gasp beneath his breath.

Place the ice axe. Step down. Place the ice axe. Step down. Lean into the wind.

From time to time I checked my watch: 2 a.m. … 4 a.m. The hours seemed to be crawling past at a cruelly slow pace, marked only by our own deterioration. We didn't even have any proper landmarks to fix on, but since the terrain had steepened again I guessed we were close to the col. Our world contained just raging wind and driving snow. And a ghostly strip of rope, heading down into the void.

Finally, just as I was beginning to fall asleep on my feet, a hint of daylight touched the night sky. Suddenly the steep terrain ended. I breathed a sigh of relief as the angle of the ground eased off. The debris of one of the lower camps was visible through the storm clouds. We had made it to the fixed ropes on the ridge.

Karma was on the point of collapse. He had given everything to get off the mountain and had nothing left in the tank. He slumped down on to the ice.

'No more walking,' he said faintly. I could see his jacket was stained; he had been bleeding heavily through the night.

At that moment four figures came out of the blizzard. Burly looking men. I feared they were soldiers. Then I saw they were wild-looking Tibetans, wrapped up in heavy yak hide coats and sheepskin hats.

Tashi took a step towards them, her face brightening.

'Nuru!' she cried.

The lead man smiled broadly.

'The international team told us about your rescue,' he said. 'We came to help.'

Tashi embraced the men warmly. Karma waved at them from his position prone on the ice. Tashi beamed at me with an expression of weary joy.

'They are monks,' Tashi told me. 'Friends of mine from the monastery.'

One of them was carrying a long object. He began to unravel it with his companion. It was a stretcher.

That was when I realised Karma had a fighting chance.

CHAPTER 11

'We need to get back to Base Camp,' Tashi said. 'Without getting discovered.'

I unfolded my map of the Everest region. We huddled down in a group to keep out the wind.

'It is possible,' Nuru said. He traced a line along the side of the valley wall with his finger. 'There's a high route here. We can miss all the checkpoints.'

We placed Karma gently on to the stretcher. The four sturdy monks lifted him up.

'Ok,' Nuru announced. 'Let's go.'

We did a big detour to avoid the main camping area at the foot of the col, then followed a faint yak herder's track across the glacier.

As we went, Nuru explained to Tashi that her parents had already left Tibet. They had rushed for the border as soon as they heard Chen had found out about Karma.

'They managed to bribe a border guard,' Nuru told Tashi. 'We heard they made it to a refugee camp in Nepal.'

Tashi thanked him for the news. She looked relieved to know her parents were safe.

Nuru and his friends set a fast pace. A couple of Western climbers went past us, but we drew little response beyond a curt 'hello'. The earthquake had created so many victims that another team with a stretcher was no surprise.

By afternoon we were weaving through the ice pinnacles, trekking through them for a few hours before starting the climb up the valley wall.

'This is a secret trail,' Tashi explained. 'Only a handful of the monks know about it.'

We took it in turns to help with the stretcher, changing our positions every ten minutes. The weight was punishing but manageable, so long as we kept rotating between us. The cloud continued to cloak us.

Just before nightfall, we stopped for a breather. One of Nuru's mates produced some bread and cold rice. We shovelled it down ravenously, caring little for the lack of taste, just intent on getting the calories inside us.

Then it was back on the slog. One foot in front of the other, taking turn after turn on the stretcher.

As darkness fell we were pretty well halfway, Nuru said.

Karma was as brave as ever. Even when he was jolted around on the stretcher he never complained. I gave him an occasional painkiller, but his shoulder must have been agony.

Tashi was exhausted; she stumbled often on the rocky terrain and took a long time to rise.

Both of us were close to the limit after our lightning raid on to Everest.

The trail became faint, a slender hint of a pathway which looked as if it had been abandoned many years before. By 2 a.m. the cloud was gone and there was no moon. We were forced to slow down as we found ourselves moving in total darkness.

I followed on wearily, my legs numb with pain. I no longer had the strength to help with the stretcher.

Some time later, Tashi gripped my arm. 'There's the lights of Base Camp,' she said.

I squinted into the darkness, my heart sinking as I saw the tiny pinpoints, miles and miles away.

'How many hours?' I asked her.

'Don't think about hours,' she said. 'Just think about

keeping going.'

Nuru and the others trekked on.

I felt my throat seizing up. The raging thirst was back. I stuffed handfuls of snow into my mouth. It was cool but did little to help.

My mind began to wander. I felt suspended halfway between reality and dream. Only by placing the shrine bell in my hand did I find the strength to continue. Thinking about my friends Kami and Shreeya helped me.

We began to descend. It was a couple of hours before daylight. The trail dropped fast towards the valley floor, twisting in a series of zigzags. I could see expedition tents scattered across the moraine.

Shapes loomed up in front of us. Freezing breath crystallising on the frigid air. Yaks.

'We're getting close,' Tashi said excitedly. 'Keep going, Ryan. Keep going!'

△

At long last we reached the yak herders zone at Base Camp, where dark figures were waiting anxiously. Tashi greeted friends as Karma was placed gently on the ground.

'We have to go,' Nuru said. He kept his voice low, not wanting to alert any guards that might be snooping around.

Karma and Tashi thanked the four monks profusely. I also embraced Nuru and his companions, thinking how incredible it had been to have their help. Of the risks they had taken.

The monks said their goodbyes, melting into the night.

Tashi and her friends began an urgent conversation. As they spoke, a darkened truck pulled up alongside their tent. A nervous looking driver poked his head out of the cab. His accent was Indian.

'I can't hang around,' he said. 'Get a move on.'

'These friends are making a dash for the Nepal border,' Tashi explained to me. 'Bribing their way through. Going into exile like my parents. Karma and I are going with them. We can drop you on the Nepali side if you wish.'

I nodded. I had to get out of Tibet somehow.

Tashi and two others dragged a large tin trunk from a tent. I helped them to manhandle it into the back of the truck.

'Faster!' the driver urged. 'Come on! The troops will catch us!'

Suddenly Tashi gasped.

'My camera! It's still in the store.'

Karma groaned.

'Leave it, Tashi … '

'There's no time,' the driver said urgently. 'We have to go now!'

He started the engine.

'Get on the truck!' I told Tashi. 'You can always get another camera.'

'I can't leave it!' She sprinted away across the moraine, heading for the angular shape of the store hut.

The truck driver shook his head. 'We're out of time. Look!'

I spun around; saw the bobbing lights of head torches, coming towards us fast.

It had to be Chen and his men.

'Tashi come back!' Karma hissed, but she kept heading for the hut.

'I go right now!' the Indian driver said. 'Are you coming or not?'

The other Tibetans climbed into the back, helping Karma to join them.

'She can still make it,' I urged the driver. 'Just a few more seconds.'

'Wait a bit longer!' insisted Karma.

A shout rang out.

The driver threw my pack down from the cab. The truck lurched forward, Karma and the other Tibetans crying out for him to stop.

I hurried for cover, hiding behind some bales of hay as angry voices called.

It all happened so fast. One moment the truck was there, the next it was gone. I could see a commotion by the store hut. By the light of Chen's head torch I saw Tashi pulled from the shadows.

She's been captured.

Chen raised something above his head then dashed it violently to the ground in a tinkle of breaking glass.

Tashi's camera.

I sank back into the darkness, my heart beating fit to burst. Tashi was hauled away to Chen's tent. The truck raced wildly into the night. I slunk away further, ducking behind a boulder some distance from the camp.

Soldiers buzzed around for a while but no one checked my hiding place. I waited for an hour, then trekked into the night, heading up a high ridge and dropping down into a valley on the far side.

At daybreak I found a nomadic encampment. They brought me in and gave me butter tea and flatbread.

I walked for the rest of the day, climbing two valley walls and then crossing a wide meltwater river which was so cold it left me with numb toes.

Late afternoon clouds were sweeping in from the south

as I caught my first sight of the small monastery. It sat at the confluence of two river systems, above a verdant green meadow. I had no idea what monastery it was, or whether they could help me, but I had no choice but to throw myself on the mercy of the monks.

I was taken to a side entrance where a young monk advised me to leave my boots. I shuffled into the main part of the temple, my eyes adjusting to the low light as I heard the murmur of mantras being recited.

The lama was an elderly monk by the name of Tsering. He greeted me in the assembly hall, a room lined with woven tapestries and dark paintings of demons. Decades of smoke from butter lamps had stained the cedar wood of the interior completely black, and I could see the ghostly shine of three vast bronze bells hanging from the rafters.

'How can I help you?' the lama asked.

Tsering listened closely as I explained my story, nodding frequently and asking occasional questions. He was particularly interested in the role of Nuru and his friends, and I realised he knew them well.

'Stay for as long as you need,' he said finally. 'You will not be bothered here.'

I was shown to a simple room with a sleeping mat and washing bowl. And there I rested my head, more weary than I had ever been in my life. Sleep was still elusive though. I was too worried about Tashi. What would become of her now? I had to find out.

My journey was not yet over. In fact the most dangerous part was about to begin.

△

It took five days for Tsering's spy to get me news about Tashi's whereabouts. Five anxious days in which I recovered from my Everest epic and ate enough to feed an army.

'They have taken your friend to a detention camp two hours to the east,' the lama told me. 'It's a notorious place, mainly filled with political prisoners.'

His words seemed to cause the air in the monastery to chill even more than normal. I shivered as I thought about Tashi behind bars. Vulnerable. At the mercy of brutal guards.

'They say that Base Camp Commander Chen is a friend of the prison chief,' he added. 'That's why she was taken to that particular place.'

'Oh.'

We began to speak. I had a hundred things to ask the monk: how would Tashi be treated in the prison? Would she actually be tried by a court, or just locked away? Would they feed her? When was she likely to be released?

'I wish I could answer your questions,' Tsering replied with regret. 'But these places are a mystery to the people of Tibet. The Chinese are extremely secretive about them. All we know is that Tibetan people can be held for years before they are released. And that sometimes they are never seen again.'

'Show me where it is on the map,' I begged him.

He pointed out the location of the detention centre, far from any main roads in the middle of nowhere.

'Do you think I can get there?'

Tsering gave me a probing look.

'What have you got in mind?' he asked.

'I don't know … ' The truth was I really *didn't* know; I just wasn't going to walk away and leave Tashi in the lurch like this. 'Maybe I can get a photo of her, make some publicity online, get a campaign going to get her released.'

Tsering nodded.

'You'd need a sympathetic contact to help you,' he said.

'Do you know someone?'

Tsering thought for a while.

'There are people I can talk to,' he said. 'Give me a little more time.'

Everything went quiet for three days. Then Tsering called me in.

'There is a man called Zhong who knows a lot about this detention camp,' he said. 'We can help you to go and meet him.'

'How?' I asked. 'Won't I get stopped at a roadblock?'

'We have a delivery service which comes in once a week,' Tsering said. 'I can ask the driver to take you. The truck goes back empty so it never normally gets checked.'

'Sounds good to me.'

'The driver can drop you at a roadway cafe where you can try and make contact with Zhong.'

We shook hands on it.

'You will leave tomorrow,' Tsering said.

I just had to go for it and trust to my luck.

△

The truck arrived first thing the next morning and negotiations began. The driver was initially reluctant but he soon changed his mind when a fifty-dollar note came out of my wallet and got waved around.

'You will go via the mountain route,' Tsering said. 'There are no police checks that way.'

I jammed myself into the vehicle cab along with some jovial Tibetan traders who were along for the ride. Then came the mountain ascent and my palms began to sweat.

The driver was slinging the truck around like a rally car, one hand on the steering wheel and the other occupied with a meat pie from which he took the occasional bite.

The vehicle raced upwards, cruising on the edge of spectacular drops, bumping through potholes that could have swallowed a yak. The Tibetans started to sing a jolly song.

For every second the driver spent looking where he was going, he spent ten seconds staring at his nails, twiddling the radio knob, or simply enjoying the view.

'Lhasa, monastery, Lhasa, monastery, no sleep,' he suddenly blurted out.

His words made me even more nervous. Lhasa to the monastery had to be a good five hundred miles, I reckoned. Was it really possible that this driver had done the trip twice without sleep? Certainly the man's eyes were bloodshot. He did look utterly exhausted.

A massive truck came thundering past, heading downhill at crazy speed. The driver swung the wheel at the final second, the truck whistling past, horn blaring, with just inches to spare. I muttered a prayer. The sooner this ride was over, the happier I would be.

Suddenly he stopped.

'Checkpoint coming!' he said. 'You out!'

I took my place in the back, covered up by some old sacking. We passed through two checkpoints without incident, except for my hip being smashed around on the metal floor.

Sometime mid-afternoon, just as my bones felt they were about to be shaken clear out of my body, we entered a small town. The air smelled of wood smoke and exhaust fumes. I heard voices calling, then the driver pulled to a halt and whistled me an all clear.

I threw off the sacking and jumped into the quiet back-street he had chosen.

△

It was perfect. There was no one around. The driver pointed the way to the tea shop which was my destination and then leapt into the cab and raced away.

I walked through the streets, checking out this town which seemed to be mostly a truckers' pit stop. The place felt dodgy, a shabby collection of cheap boarding houses and roadside mechanics' shacks arranged along a meandering main street.

Small groups of dark-clad men were huddled together smoking in the alleyways that flanked the muddy road. Chinese police were everywhere, cruising up and down in squad cars every few minutes.

The tea room was right on the main Lhasa road, a stopping off place for tourist groups and long-distance buses. The restaurant was busy serving steaming bowls of vegetables and rice. I ordered some food and watched the scene for a while, trying to work out who was in charge.

After a bit it became clear that the boss was the elderly woman sitting behind the till. She spent most of her time moaning at the waiters, but beneath her strict exterior I detected a kindly side to her character.

I walked up to her, my heart hammering in my chest.

'I'm looking for a man called Zhong,' I told her.

'Zhong? Not here.'

Phew. So they knew about him at least.

'Could I get a message to him? I would like to meet.'

The old lady looked at me with a keen expression, obviously sussing me out.

'It's important,' I added. 'I think he will want to meet me.'

'Maybe,' she said cautiously. 'I will send a boy to try and find him.'

I sat in the tea shop through most of that day, writing up my diary and trying to keep my nerves under control. I felt like a character in a spy thriller, waiting for this rendezvous with my mysterious contact.

Finally, Zhong arrived.

To my amazement he didn't look Tibetan at all. He looked Chinese.

He was surprisingly young, in his late twenties I reckoned, with keenly intelligent eyes and neatly combed hair. His clothes were those of a Western youth, jeans, sweatshirt and jacket. He shook my hand then looked around the room at the other customers.

'Better we go to the kitchen,' he said.

He led me through a swing door into the steamy interior of the shack where we found some space at a table.

'How did you hear about me?' he asked. His English was excellent.

I told him about Tsering, about the map that had alerted me to where Tashi was being held.

'Can I see the map? he asked.

He scrutinised it closely, turning it in his hands.

'It is correct,' Zhong said. 'This camp does exist, even though the authorities try to keep it secret.'

'How do you know so much about it?' I asked him.

Zhong made eye contact with me for long seconds. I got the sense he was making a momentous decision. Then he sipped his tea and spoke quietly.

'I'm a military guard at the camp.'

The kitchen door swung open with a crash as a Tibetan man entered. Zhong stiffened, then relaxed as the man nodded at him.

'A *guard*?'

I stared at Zhong with my mouth open. I had never imagined my secret contact would be Chinese, let alone a member of the Chinese *military*. He was taking crazy risks. Or was this a trap?

I sipped my tea, trying to stop my hand from trembling, suddenly very unsure of the situation. I might be talking to a Chinese spy.

'I can guess what you're thinking,' Zhong said earnestly. 'But don't worry. You can trust me.'

He nodded at me encouragingly and I felt he was sincere.

'Is it possible to go there?' I asked him. 'If I can get a photo of the place Tashi's being held, maybe I can make some publicity about what's happened.'

He nodded.

'I can take you. It won't be the first time I've guided people there.'

'What if we get caught?' I asked. 'What will happen to you if your bosses know you've done this?'

Zhong looked grave.

'Better we don't talk about that,' he said.

I felt a strong urge to ask him why he was doing this, about his decision to help the Tibetans. But I guessed it would be difficult or even dangerous for him to tell me more.

'We can go to the camp tonight,' he said. 'We'll have to borrow a motorbike.'

We walked out of the village to a tented herders' encampment where Zhong was greeted like a long-lost son. An elderly shepherd offered us salted tea and biscuits and agreed to lend his motorbike without a moment's hesitation.

'We leave at ten tonight,' Zhong said.

△

We entered the shepherd's tent and spent some hours resting on piles of blankets as the afternoon wore on. Three shy children came to visit, poking their heads round the embroidered doorway, their eyes wide with curiosity.

Zhong and I talked. I told him more about Tashi, about the problems her family had had with Captain Chen.

At the mention of Chen's name, Zhong went pale. I saw his fingers curl into a fist. I waited for him to open up but he kept silent. I got the strong impression that Zhong knew about Chen.

'Why did you decide to help the Tibetans?' I asked.

'I've seen the truth about how they are treated,' Zhong said. 'I just want to do my bit to help. Show that not all Chinese people are the same.'

The sun dropped beneath the flank of a neighbouring hill. The temperature plummeted.

'Time to go,' he told me. Zhong had borrowed some Tibetan clothes from the shepherd by way of a disguise.

'OK.'

I clambered on to the rear of the bike and we zoomed up a switchback trail, rising quickly in a series of steep zigzags above the plateau and then crossing a bleak col where a gale-force blast almost blew us off the road.

'Windy as usual!' Zhong shouted.

He didn't use the headlights. And neither of us was wearing a crash helmet. I tried to put that out of my mind.

The cold ripped through me as the motorbike accelerated. The night air was already below zero and the wind chill drove icy daggers into every inch of my body.

'Lights!' Zhong cried out. He veered off the track and killed the engine.

An army truck thundered past.

Zhong waited until the lorry was gone then kicked the motorbike into life. We rode back to the track and a further hour of the white-knuckle ride followed. From time to time we passed the dark rectangular shapes of shepherds' tents, the night air filling briefly with the sharp scent of goats and sheep. Once or twice we were chased by ferocious dogs, snapping at the rear wheel for sport.

Then came a distant luminous glow.

'That's the lights of the prison,' Zhong called. 'We'll go on foot from here.'

We hid the bike behind a boulder and began to trek along the side of the road. I was grateful for the activity after sitting still on the ride, the chill in my bones easing as we walked.

'There's a military post up ahead,' Zhong told me quietly, pointing to a small wooden shack. 'We have to keep absolutely silent now.'

We passed just twenty metres from the hut. Close enough that we could hear the murmur of male voices inside, smell the distinctive aroma of burning dung and cheap tobacco in the smoke that trickled from the chimney.

Then came the sound of a door opening. A sudden spill of light. A burst of tinny Chinese pop music. Footsteps crunched across the ice. We crouched down as low as we could, using a frozen bank of snow for cover. I felt my heart racing with the fear of discovery.

The soldier walked ten or fifteen paces across the field and began to pee. A cigarette butt arced through the air and hit the ground in a flurry of orange sparks. I held my breath.

There was a long pause. Had the soldier seen something suspicious? The moment stretched out horribly.

Then came the sound of footsteps again. The door slamming shut. A minute later we were past the shack and climbing up the slope behind it.

For almost an hour we ascended the hillside. Zhong set a steady pace and I concentrated on matching him step for step.

'Now we go slowly,' Zhong whispered. 'Keep low.'

We crawled up to the ridgeline and cautiously peeped over the top.

'There you are,' Zhong said. 'Detention Camp 43.'

Down in the bottom of the valley, lit by arc lights, was this nightmare of a place, a collection of scruffy grey concrete buildings surrounded by barbed wire barriers. The structures looked agricultural, each one about the size of a farmyard barn.

'The men are held in the one on the left.' Zhong said. 'Your friend is in the building on the right.'

'How many prisoners are there?' I asked.

'About sixty or seventy. It's hard to say because it's all run on the whim of the camp commander. There's hardly any paperwork, a lot of them haven't had any proper trial.'

I felt a wave of anger rising inside me.

'The world should know about this.'

'Yes,' Zhong nodded. 'It's a dumping ground for human beings. Many of them are here because of their religious convictions. I talk to them, that's why I decided to help.'

A few guards were visible, sitting around a table in the yard. It was hard to see properly at such a long distance, but it looked like they were playing cards.

'How can I get a photo of my friend?' I asked.

'Only one way,' Zhong said. I could see his eyes glittering in the moonlight. 'We go in and find her.'

'Go in?' my whole body shivered at the thought of the risk.

'Yes. I know the ways to dodge the security.'

Zhong looked at me keenly.

'Are you up for it?'

'Sure.'

And that was when things started getting really interesting.

CHAPTER 12

'The guards will start going to sleep soon,' Zhong whispered. 'We'll have to wait a bit.'

The cold began to bite. Within ten minutes I was shivering and I could tell that even my guide was feeling it. To distract myself I thought about how close I was to seeing Tashi again.

'There's the main guard, in the watchtower,' Zhong said.

A solitary figure paced to and fro, evidently trying to keep warm. We saw the flare of a match and the bitter smell of rough tobacco reached us on the night breeze. A couple of men emerged with towels in their hands. They crossed to the wash block, talking animatedly.

'There's your friend Chen,' Zhong whispered.

My hackles rose. I hadn't expected to see him at the camp.

'You know him, don't you?'

Zhong made a strange noise in his throat.

'He's got family working here, comes here quite a bit. And the camp boss is his oldest friend.'

Later a man came out with some sort of wheeled dust-bin. He tipped the contents into a rubbish skip and went back inside. A couple of feral dogs emerged from the shadows and began scavenging for the scraps that hadn't made it into the skip. The watchtower guard wrapped a couple of heavy blankets around his shoulders.

The cold continued to assault us but gradually the lights went off. The camp was shutting down for the night and by 2 a.m. all was quiet. The guard in the tower was nowhere to be seen. He had ducked down for some kip by the looks of it.

'OK,' Zhong said. 'Let's begin.'

We descended the slope and reached the perimeter wall of the camp. All my senses were on high alert, expecting a cry of alarm from the watchtower at any second ... But all was silent.

We began to creep along the wall, making our way as quietly as we could. The moon was up high now, casting a silvery light over the valley in a way that was both helpful and a pain in the neck.

A whole range of terrible fears attacked me as we got closer to the compound. What if we were walking into a trap? And a new terror. What if the troops started shooting? We would be two shadows invading the camp. Nobody would have any idea who we were. We could be thieves. Terrorists. A trigger-happy guard might be within his rights to shoot first and ask questions later.

Thoughts like this crowded in, swirling round my head and ramping up the fear. I faltered and stopped. I was on the point of turning to Zhong and telling him I couldn't go through with it.

'What's wrong?' Zhong whispered. 'You OK?'

Then I thought about Tashi; how courageous she had been on Everest. The way she had been so focussed on saving her brother. And it helped me. I got through the moment of doubt.

'It's alright,' I told Zhong. 'Let's keep going.'

We resumed the progress along the wall and after a short time we reached a spot where it had partially collapsed. It wasn't a big hole but it would be enough for us to squeeze through.

'I'll go first,' Zhong said.

Zhong darted across the yard and took cover behind one of the trucks. He became invisible in the shadows. Nothing stirred, there was no cry of alarm. No one had seen him. I waited a minute or so and then ran across to join him, my heart vibrating inside my chest at a frequency I had never known before.

So far so good. We were within a stone's throw of the building that was marked on the map.

'Go!' Zhong hissed.

This time we moved together, sprinting side by side across a basketball court and making it to the block. Seconds later we were standing at the doorway and listening for sounds from the interior. Nothing. Our luck was holding.

Zhong gently pulled down the handle. I was expecting it to be locked but it swung open as he pushed it. He smiled at me in the darkness.

We entered the building, finding ourselves in a long corridor with a number of doors set off it. I was aware that one could open at any minute, wrecking everything. We just stood there in silence, letting our eyes adjust to the low light.

'The cells are at the far end of the corridor,' Zhong whispered. 'Go and find your friend. I'll keep guard. If I see someone coming I'll give you a sign.'

I made my way down the corridor, treading as quietly as I could. The most terrifying thing was not knowing what was behind those anonymous doors. Each one I passed felt like a ticking time bomb ready to explode.

The final door had been replaced with bars so that the room was converted into a cell. In the corner I could just make out a bed. A figure was huddled up inside, breathing steadily and deeply. I waited for a few moments to assess the situation, wondering if it was really her or not.

'Hey!' I hissed. 'Tashi?'

Nothing happened. I tried the same call again, a tiny bit louder. The figure stirred, a head of jet-black hair emerging from the blankets.

'Ryan?'

Tashi jumped out of the bed and rushed towards me, blinking sleep out of her eyes and smiling like crazy.

'You came!' she whispered. Our fingers interlocked through the bars. We held each other as best we could, both trying to keep tears away.

'You crazy idiot,' she laughed. 'If they catch you in here … ?'

An engine suddenly started up in the yard outside. Tashi pulled back and for a moment she was illuminated by the sweeping beam of the searchlight. The engine died.

I brought out my camera.

'Let me take a photo,' I whispered. 'I can get it distributed by news agencies, raise publicity and get you freed.'

'Are you nuts?' she said. 'I'm not interested in a photo. I need you to help me *escape*. Right here and right now.'

And I knew from her eyes that she really wasn't kidding.

△

I don't mind admitting I had a slight panic attack at that point. Breaking into the camp had already been by a factor of ten the most outrageous thing I'd ever done. But helping Tashi to escape? That was never in the game plan. Not in my wildest dreams.

I think I just stood there in shock for a bit with my mouth wide open. It felt like I was already in too deep. But … but something inside me could see the true nature of Tashi's situation. She was totally vulnerable, subject to the whims and moods of the camp commander and his friend Chen – a volatile monster with a capacity for harm.

He could kill Tashi at any moment and 'vanish' the body into a shallow grave somewhere in the loneliest country on the planet.

'OK. Let's say we get this cell open,' I said, 'and we get out of the camp. Where do you think we can go from there?'

'I have no idea,' Tashi admitted, 'I'm making this up as I go along.'

'It's a thousand kilometres to Lhasa. The military can stop any vehicle they like. They'll catch us easily.'

'Look. Will you just stop *thinking* and get on with it,' she said.

I ran down the corridor and told Zhong about Tashi's proposal. I was expecting him to throw up his hands in horror and tell me it was crazy, that we shouldn't risk it in a million years. But I should have known better; what he actually did was break into a big smile and say,

'Great idea! Let's get her out of here!'

Zhong led me a short way, checking the door plaques as we went.

'This is a tool room,' he said. He tried the handle and found it was locked. He inspected the mechanism and winked at me, saying, 'It's not very strong.'

He took another look out into the yard to check no one was about. Then he took three steps away from the storeroom door and simply shoulder charged it as hard as he could. The lock gave way with a splintering sound of wood and a rendering of metal. His shoulder charge had broken the whole hinge and the door was swinging free. We waited to see if the noise had alerted anyone.

Nothing stirred.

'No problem!' he whispered.

The store room was an Aladdin's cave. A selection of tools was hanging on one of the walls and Zhong lost no time in selecting what he wanted.

'Bolt cutters!' he said. 'These should do the job.'

I took the tool from him. It weighed a ton. I ran back down the corridor to Tashi's cell and her face cracked up in a smile as she saw what we'd found.

'Perfect!' she hissed.

I lifted the bolt cutters up and positioned them so the sharp blades at the end were snug around the right part of the padlock.

'Quickly!' Tashi urged. 'Let's do it before the next patrol comes round.'

For a while it felt like nothing was happening, then, little by little, as I squeezed the two prongs of the handles towards each other, I felt the metal shaft of the padlock beginning to give way.

'It's working,' Tashi said excitedly. 'I can see the metal cutting.'

Then, with a metallic 'ping' noise, the padlock snapped in two.

'Yes!' I put the bolt cutters down and wiggled the

broken lock free. Seconds later the door was swinging open. Tashi stepped into the corridor and sprang straight into my arms, hugging me tighter than I'd ever been hugged before.

'Thank you,' she whispered.

Zhong walked up the corridor and picked up the bolt cutters.

'Result!' I said. 'Now let's get out of here.'

'Not so fast,' Zhong replied. 'We're not done yet.'

I got a spasm of nerves.

'How do you mean?' I whispered, every fibre of my body itching to get out of that camp.

'Since we've got these cutters,' he said. 'We should free the rest of the prisoners.'

My heart sank as deep as it could go at that point. It felt like we had already pushed our luck to the very far edges of what we could get away with. But to free more prisoners? Was he really *serious*?

I looked at Tashi, desperately wanting her to intervene, persuade Zhong to abandon the idea, to tell him that we had to get out while we still could.

'It's a great plan,' she said.

I should have known better again. Of course Tashi would want to help free her fellow Tibetans.

'They're in that building over there,' Zhong pointed to the largest of the hangars.

'Guards!' Tashi exclaimed. She had seen movement through the window. We ducked down beneath the sill as the murmur of voices reached us. We stayed motionless for several minutes, praying that the men wouldn't come to check the corridor.

An engine fired into life, swiftly followed by the roar of a jeep moving away. We heard the clang of the compound gates being swung back and the sound of the vehicle driving off down the valley. Zhong poked his head above the sill.

'All clear,' he said. 'Let's move over there, see if we can get in.'

Zhong took the lead, hurrying across to a couple of fuel tankers parked to the side of the parade ground. We used them as cover, sneaking silently behind them, out of sight of the watchtower. Once we reached the hangar building we kept tight to the wall, pressing into the darkest shadows as we headed for the doors at the end.

A strange howl echoed round the valley. The hairs on the back of my neck prickled. A fox was out there in the frozen night, calling for a mate. The camp remained quiet.

'That's the guardhouse,' Zhong whispered. 'I'll go and take a look.'

He bent down low, creeping right underneath the frosted window. I became aware of a low rhythmic sound coming from the hut. He waited a minute or so then raised his head slowly above the sill, peering into the hut for a moment then ducking back down and returning to where we waited in the shadows.

'One guard,' he murmured. 'Fast asleep.'

That explained the sound. The man was snoring.

We sprinted the final ten metres to the detention building, bundling through the door and closing it quietly behind us.

The layout was very different to the block that Tashi had been held in. There were no individual cells here, just an iron mesh barrier with a vast open space behind it in which rows of bunk beds had been built.

'This is the men's section,' Zhong whispered.

We padded quietly down the corridor, Zhong in the lead.

'Hey!' he hissed. 'Wake up!'

Figures began to stir in the bunks. Blankets were tossed aside, dishevelled-looking Tibetans shuffled barefoot across the concrete floor towards us.

'What's happening?'

'We're getting you out of here,' Zhong told the men. He fixed the bolt cutters to the padlock and squeezed the handles with all his strength. The shaft snapped apart as more of the prisoners emerged from the darkness, rubbing their eyes and trying to work out what was going on. The door sprung open. The men stared at us with suspicion, evidently wondering if this was some sort of trap.

Zhong addressed them in their own language and the mood changed completely. A sense of urgency overtook the prisoners as they ran back to the bunks to wake up their friends.

'They're going to make a run for it,' Zhong explained.

He was approached by several of the inmates, greeted with embraces, warm words and smiles.

The prisoners were swarming down the corridor. In a matter of seconds all of them had left their bunks, pulling on their shoes and boots, desperate to take their chance for escape. The noise was incredible. By the time the captives hit the parade ground the whole camp would be awake. A feeling of utter dread began to engulf me. I had the terrible sensation this situation was now primed to end in a bloodbath.

We sprinted down the corridor. Tumbled into the parade ground. The guard in the box was well and truly awake, blowing on a whistle and shouting blue murder. The prisoners were scattering in all possible directions, each seemingly with their own idea of how to get out of the camp. A running Tibetan pushed the guard roughly to the ground and the whistling stopped.

'This way!' Zhong told us. He made a beeline for the other side of the square.

Back at the main block I could see figures rushing about. Some were dashing towards the security fence, pulling at the barbed wire and quickly bringing it down. Other prisoners were hurrying towards the main gates where two young guards were standing with their mouths open, their guns still slung on their shoulders, obviously unsure what to do. A siren went off. More soldiers began to spill out of the shacks, pulling on their uniforms as they hit the freezing night air.

'If they start shooting it's going to be a massacre,' Tashi said fearfully.

'Keep moving,' Zhong said. He led the way, heading across the camp for the gap in the fence that had let us in.

A hijacked jeep drove past at high speed, two of the escaped Tibetans in the front. The soldiers fired a handful of bullets but failed to hit the men. They did hit a tyre however and the prisoners jumped out and ran for the perimeter fence as the vehicle limped to a halt. It was chaos.

Then came flames. An army truck had erupted in a ball of fire.

'They want to destroy this place,' Zhong said. 'Make sure no more Tibetans can ever be locked up here again.'

The fire was spreading fast. A second truck also started to blaze. Soldiers rushed for fire extinguishers, began to spray the vehicles, trying to calm the flames.

'Stop!' a voice screamed through a megaphone.

I saw Chen and the camp commander emerge from a hut.

Then came a sound like a firework. Two flares suddenly arched high into the night sky. They soared towards the heavens for a few seconds then began to parachute back to earth, burning with a ferociously bright phosphorous light. The entire camp was illuminated. We had lost the advantage of darkness. A soldier spotted us taking cover by a truck. He began to chatter into his walkie-talkie.

'The fence!' Zhong hissed. 'Go!'

He pushed us out from behind the truck and we sprinted as fast as we could across the parade ground. There was no point in trying to hide now, we just ran blindly for the escape route, my back tingling with the thoroughly unpleasant sensation that a bullet might shatter my spine at any second.

We pounded towards the break in the fence. A round whistled over our heads. Boots were thudding into the ground behind us. I turned to flash a look back. Five or six soldiers were on our trail.

Zhong's sense of direction had been faultless. We hit the fence exactly at the right spot. Tashi squirmed through and I followed her as fast as I could, ripping my jacket on some razor wire in my desperation to get out. Zhong was the last one through.

We ran blindly up the far slope, legs pounding into the dirt, lungs burning in the thin air. A hundred metres of sprinted height-gain took us all to the point of exhaustion and we halted in a huddle, staring back at the perimeter fence.

'They stopped,' Tashi said.

'Trying to block the others from leaving,' Zhong said.

We continued to the top of the rise. The camp was about two hundred metres below us, many of the buildings ablaze. The troops were still running round like headless chickens, trying to extinguish the flames.

We saw an overhang cut into the nearby cliff. Zhong pulled us into the protection of the small cave and we had an urgent whispered conference to try to decide what to do next.

'We have to get to a town,' I proposed. 'As fast as possible. Try and talk to some Western journalists, tell the truth about what's happened.'

Zhong sucked in his breath.

'There are no Western journalists in Tibet,' he said glumly. 'They've all been banned by the government.'

'How about we get hold of a vehicle?' I asked. 'Drive to the border and escape?'

'That won't work,' he said. 'There's only two towns within a hundred kilometres of here and they're both crawling with spies. As soon as we set foot in those places, we'll be arrested.'

An explosion split the air down in the camp. Yells rang out.

'There's only one way out of this,' Tashi said. 'We have to make a dash for the border. Cross illegally into Nepal.'

I pulled out my map, switched on my head torch.

'There's a secret crossing point here,' Zhong said, stabbing at the river that formed the border. 'I've been down there on patrol and seen Tibetans using it.'

I felt my breath quicken. Nepal meant safety. Could we really do it? Get into the country illegally? And what would happen if we were caught sneaking across?

'Are there guards down there?' I asked.

'No. No border fence or anything. The authorities rely on the river as a natural barrier. It's white water. Dangerous currents.'

'How far is it?' Tashi asked.

Zhong thought for a while, then replied. 'Twenty kilometres, I guess.'

'When you say that river is dangerous ... ' I asked. 'What are we talking on a scale of one to ten?'

'Ten, if you try to swim it,' Zhong said. 'But I saw a secret smugglers' place last time I was on patrol. A spot where a couple of old boats are stored.'

We all fell silent. No one said anything. It was clear our options had come down to this single desperate plan: an illegal crossing into Nepal. Across a raging river.

'They're coming!' Tashi suddenly said.

I spun around, saw two of the soldiers pushing through the gap. Then a larger figure came through behind, joining them as they ran up the slope towards us.

Chen.

We hurried away from the cave.

CHAPTER 13

We moved swiftly down the far side of the hill, heading for a plain which looked vast and forbidding in the moonlight. Zhong led the way with confidence and I was grateful for that. With no compass between us it was essential that someone knew the direction to go in.

For an hour we kept up a crazy pace, half trekking, half jogging across the terrain. I was hoping that the commander and his soldiers would give up, but they just kept on coming.

'They're getting closer,' Zhong said. His eyesight seemed to be better than ours. All I could see was vague dots moving at a great distance. Tashi and I looked at each other. Then we saw a green flash, followed by a strange glow.

'Night vision goggles!' Zhong said grimly. 'It means they can see us plain as day.'

'Let's pick up more speed!' Tashi urged.

We pushed as hard as we could, hard enough that I could feel the muscles in my legs beginning to tighten and protest. Tashi was the strongest of us, striding powerfully onwards, never showing signs of tiring.

Midnight came and went. Our pursuers maintained their relentless march. A vicious thirst began to overwhelm me, but all of the streams were frozen. I kept a careful eye on the luminous dial of my watch, ticking off the hours to try and keep a fix on our progress.

Three hours later I was trying to work out how much distance we had covered. I knew it was possible to walk at five or six kilometres an hour. On the flat. I figured we were slower. We were having to navigate round lots of obstacles. There were multiple hills to get over. Small iced-up streams that had to be crossed. Larger peaks that had to be circled. The terrain was rocky and unpredictable. Every step required concentration.

The sound of rushing water punched through the silence of the night. We came to a river as wide as a city road. The flow was enough to keep the river from freezing. We kneeled, scooping the precious water up with our hands.

It was cold enough to burn our throats but we kept on drinking, aware that this might be our last opportunity for many hours.

After removing our boots, we picked our way gingerly across the river. The stones felt sharp underfoot, digging painfully into our soles as we waded through the freezing water. I clutched my boots for grim life. The current would sweep things away in an instant if they were dropped.

We used handfuls of wiry grass to dry off our feet. Then it was back on the march, our river-frozen toes gradually thawing out as blood began to flow.

At 3 a.m. the sky was as crisp and clear as any I had ever seen. The moon had vanished, but the starlight itself was bright enough to illuminate the ground. The Milky Way stretched in a shimmering arc right across the night sky.

'We've got a star shadow,' Tashi observed with wonder. 'I didn't even know that was possible.'

She was right. Our shadows were projected on to the frozen tundra, delicate and faint. I felt a sense of privilege to be witnessing such an incredible thing. If it hadn't been for the fact we had a psychotic maniac and his henchmen on our trail, I would almost have been enjoying the whole thing.

The sense of isolation was complete. For many hours we had seen no sign of life. No shepherd tents. No glow of lights to announce a small mining operation or hamlet. The silence had been all-embracing, with only the rhythmic pattern of our breath, the crunch of our boots breaking the spell.

Only once did we see wildlife. The slinking figure of what I thought was a dog, silhouetted on a high ridgeline.

'Wolf,' Zhong said.

The creature hurried away as soon as it saw us.

By 5 a.m. I was hitting the wall, punching through one pain barrier after another as my legs began to give up. The climb on Everest had already taken me to the limit and now I was asking my body for more.

Zhong was also weaving from side to side, no longer capable of walking in a straight line. Only Tashi kept her pace fixed and I knew she was utterly focussed on one thing: joining her family in Nepal.

Finally dawn broke. A creamy, hazy light creeping across the plateau. The sky was filled with clouds. We started climbing, ascending a steep hill, my calves cramping up as we got higher.

We hit the crest.

'There!' Zhong exclaimed. 'You can see Nepal.'

Far away to the south we could see a neat village perched on a mountainside. Smoke was rising from the houses.

Brightly dressed workers were already leaving for their day's labour in the terraced fields.

'My parents ... ' Tashi whispered. 'Karma ... they are just a few hours away.'

The dawn light picked out the smile on her face.

'How far is the river?' I asked.

'One hour's walking,' Zhong said. 'Then we'll have to find a way across the rapids.'

'We'll do it,' Tashi said.

Zhong looked back across the plateau. I followed his eyeline, seeing the tiny figures of Chen and his two men still marching determinedly in our footsteps. They obviously knew we were heading for the river. Zhong pulled his hat low across his face. I guessed he didn't want to risk his identity becoming known now it was daylight.

'We have to find those boats,' he said. 'That's the vital thing now.'

△

Zhong led the way, never wavering, never faltering, aiming as straight as a die for the river.

Then, just before 7 a.m., we saw it for the first time. Far below our position. A turbulent maelstrom of white water. The sound of colliding boulders reached us. The riverbed was permanently on the move, grinding and pulverising even the biggest rocks into fragments of stone dust and sending them on their tumbling descent to the sea.

Tashi said nothing. But I could see how she felt by the way her shoulders slumped.

'It didn't look that big on the map,' she said quietly.

'We can't swim it,' I said. 'We'll die.'

I looked into the wild canyon. I had figured the river might be twenty or thirty metres across, with calmer spots where a crossing might be made. But the creature coursing through the canyon was far wider than that – the water vicious and untamed. Huge waves formed and reformed around jagged boulders in a mesmerising cycle of white-caps and spray. It would be suicide to try and cross it without a boat. After a few strokes a swimmer would be swept away, gripped by the current and spun swiftly downstream to be crushed against the rocks.

'I did warn you,' Zhong said.

We stood saying nothing as we watched the raging water, the roar of the river seeming to become more intrusive with every moment. Then we looked back across the plain at Chen and his men. It was hard to get an accurate fix on their distance but they looked frighteningly close.

'I think it's this way,' Zhong said urgently. 'We have to

get down to the water's edge.'

We hit a track, slipping and sliding on the loose ground. It funnelled us downstream. We went for ten minutes. Zhong stopped once. Then again. He stared around at the surroundings, looking uncertain.

'I don't know ... ' he said doubtfully. 'It looks different to how I remember ... '

Drips of sweat ran down my spine. The heat of the day was rising. Chen and his men were getting closer now and we were stumbling with exhaustion.

'We need to traverse more,' Zhong announced.

Tashi and I followed him, moving as fast as we dared.

The canyon was narrower than ever, squeezing the river tight. Jammed between the sheer walls, the water was forced to become ever faster and more turbulent, waves colliding haphazardly and sending huge jets of spray into the air. The roar was deafening, we could hardly hear ourselves speak.

'There's Nepal, look. So close!' Tashi pointed across the vast valley, at the village clustered on the hillside, now just a few miles distant on the other side of the river. We saw a strip of beach below us.

'That's it!' Zhong exclaimed.

'I don't see any boat ... ' Tashi said.

My heart sank. It really didn't look like there was a way down. Then I noticed a faint track zigzagging through the rocks.

'We take that path,' Zhong said. 'Follow me!'

Zhong descended, grabbing hold of handfuls of vegetation to steady himself, then dropping on to the shingle strip.

'Come and see!'

I scrambled down the canyon side, slipping and sliding, making it clumsily to the beach where our guide was standing with a manic grin on his face.

'Check it out!' he exclaimed.

A cave was set into the cliff face. Tashi joined us and at that precise moment we heard a cry.

Chen and his two henchmen were picking their way down the slope.

△

We ran into the shadowy interior of the cave. Two boats were in there. One of them was in good condition. The other had patches and the leather looked cracked.

The three of us got to work, tugging the better of the coracles out on to the beach.

'There's no paddles!' Tashi said.

Small rocks began to cascade. Chen and his men were right above us, hurrying down the track.

'Quickly!'

We dragged the coracle to the water's edge, holding on tight to the mooring rope as the current threatened to rip it out of our hands.

'Get in!' I yelled.

Tashi moved forward, clutching on to the edges for dear life as it rocked perilously from side to side. Zhong went next, finding some space next to her. I stepped in carefully, making sure I put my weight on to the wooden frame and not directly on to the leather skin. The tiny vessel felt overloaded already.

I picked up a pole from the beach and used it to push away from the shore. The coracle tilted crazily as it began to float. Water spilled over the lip but the thing floated. Just.

The current gripped us. We began to pick up speed, spinning through a complete circle as the boat lurched down a small rapid. Water began to flood into the bottom. My feet went numb as the icy river filled my boots.

'Paddle!' Tashi yelled.

We paddled with our hands, making it out into the turbulent centre of the river.

Chen jumped down to the beach. He screamed a string of furious words, then turned and saw the cave. Quick as a flash he went for the other vessel. His men helped him drag it out. Only then did the thought hit me: we should have sabotaged that second boat.

'Bail!' I cried to Tashi. I was steering by using the stick as a rudder.

Tashi cupped her hands and began to throw water out of the vessel. Seconds later I gave up attempting to steer and joined her in the effort, my hands a blur as I wildly scooped at the water.

A huge wave slapped against us. The little boat juddered, the leather skin creaking and stretching with the blow. The vessel was waterlogged, and sinking lower and lower in the river.

'Faster!' Tashi yelled.

We redoubled our efforts to bale it out.

Chen and his men had the boat out of the cave. Seconds later the commander was pushed into the ferocious current.

I began to shiver. My trousers were wet through. I could feel my inner warmth being sucked quickly away. Zhong was worse. His upper body had taken the full impact of the water and every part of him was drenched. His teeth were chattering so hard I could hear them even above the roar of the river. A jagged rock loomed up. We missed it by a whisker, the side of the tiny boat just skimming past.

Chen was getting closer. He was faster and lighter than us, bobbing in and out of view as his boat rode the waves. He pulled out his pistol and aimed it in our direction.

'Down!' Tashi screamed.

A bullet whined over our heads, the shockwave ripping past in a percussive blast of air. The canyon narrowed even further. The walls whizzing past at ridiculous speed. We were totally out of control; completely at the mercy of the thundering water.

Chen was coming ever nearer. Only the violent bucking of his boat prevented him getting off another shot.

'Watch out!' Tashi shouted.

A wave curled over us. The boat juddered as it rammed a rock. A stunning shock of pain ran through my arm. The sound of splintering wood punched through the roar of the rushing river. I blinked water out of my eyes. Zhong was gone. The leather wall of the boat was ripped. Water was gushing in much too fast to bale.

The boat sank from beneath us. Tashi sank with it. I held out my hand but she was too far off. She came up for air. I saw her snatch a breath. Then the waves pulled her away.

I spun round and just caught a glimpse of a monstrous hole in the river. I was tipped backwards, went into freefall for a brief moment, then splashed down sideways into a seething maelstrom of a hole. The boat was on top of me. Then it was ripped away by the current.

A *stopper.* Incredibly, my mind found the word. A wave that keeps circulating round and round. A wave from which escape is almost impossible.

My body rolled. Irresistible force pushed me down. I was still thinking about Tashi. I hit the riverbed, getting tumbled along and then thrust back up.

Is she OK?

I felt my lungs straining for air. I forced my eyes open, saw nothing but raging white water. My head burst clear. I snatched a breath. Half-filled my lungs, but inhaling water as well. Then it was back under. That unseen hand dragging me down again. I hit the riverbed for the second time. Stones were ripping into my back. I could feel my vision fading. My lungs were ready to explode. Then I sensed someone beside me.

Tashi?

No. Zhong. He pulled my arms. I kicked my legs out behind me as hard as I could. One foot hit a boulder, helped to push us forward. We lurched upwards, our heads bursting clear of the water as we sucked precious air into our lungs.

We were out of the stopper. Back in the flow. Battered by wave after wave as the river tossed us one way and another. The current powered us round the bend in the canyon.

'Where's Tashi?' I asked Zhong. 'Did you see what happened?'

I saw a stony beach. Trees surrounding it. I pulled on the branches with my right arm. I helped Zhong to swing around. Our feet touched the bottom and the two of us staggered forwards, coughing up water and gasping for breath.

We stood on the beach, so glad to be alive. We were in Nepal. We'd made it. But where was Tashi?

Then we heard splashing in the shallows behind us. We whipped around, praying for it to be her.

It was Chen, the gun raised in his shaking hand.

A shot rang out. Zhong fell. His body hit the stones of the little beach. Blood gushed from a wound in his chest. The world seemed to stop. I couldn't breathe. Couldn't think.

Chen strutted arrogantly towards us. Then he saw Zhong's face and his whole body shuddered.

'No ... ' Chen whispered. His face went deathly pale. He fell to his knees by Zhong's side. Zhong's lips parted.

Tashi struggled out of the river and stood by my side as our courageous Chinese friend stared directly into Chen's eyes. He half smiled. It seemed almost a look of affection. Then he uttered his last word on this earth. The very last word Tashi and I expected to hear.

'Father ... '

CHAPTER 14

THREE DAYS LATER

UNITED NATIONS REFUGEE CAMP 'DELTA'

NEPAL

The sun was setting as the funeral ceremony began. There were six of us in the mourning party: Tashi and her family, a venerable Buddhist priest and myself. We gathered in the shade of a spreading banyan tree as the heat of the day died away, united in the desire to pay our final respects to our friend.

Zhong's body lay before us, wrapped in a simple white shroud. As we watched, four monks in saffron robes arrived with a bamboo frame. They lifted the body, carrying it shoulder high and stepping in unison across the twisted roots of the banyan on to the dusty tracks of the camp.

Word about Zhong's courageous actions had spread amongst the Tibetan refugees. Almost one thousand of them lined the makeshift processional way through the camp, standing in dignified silence as the body was carried through the long rows of khaki tents.

Tashi and I were both on alert. We scanned the crowds continuously for Chen. After the shooting incident he had thrown his weapon into the river and walked away into the forest, his face a mask of despair. We had assumed he would try to cross back to Tibet, but on the day before the funeral we had been warned someone was asking around at the village close to the river, looking for information about where we had gone with the body. We had no idea what he was planning, but he was obviously on our trail.

Down by the river a cremation pyre had been built. Silken cloths of orange and gold had been draped across the cords of seasoned juniper and cedar and the air was fragrant with the sweet aromas of jasmine and sandalwood.

Children of the camp had been busy for much of the day. Their labours had produced a beautiful arch of woven jacaranda fronds, laced with purple orchids. Tashi sighed as we passed beneath it. Her hand slipped into mine.

We reached the river. The body was placed on the pyre. A flaming brand was produced. The lama chanted over it.

'Sacred fire,' Tashi whispered.

The priest stepped forward, touching the stack once, twice, three times. The flames licked skywards, dancing and crackling into life.

The smoke thickened. The heat intensified. I pulled Tashi back a couple of paces as one side of the pyre spat out a blast of superheated air. The body was quickly consumed by the flames. I felt Tashi's hand tighten on mine.

'Look,' she whispered. She pointed to the other side of the pyre.

At first I could see nothing unusual. Just the mourners. Then, through the flames and the smoke, I saw a figure detach itself from the crowd. He was dressed in simple peasant clothing and limping heavily. The river had left its mark.

Chen.

The Chinese commander stepped forward, right to the very edge of the burning logs where the heat must have been almost unbearable. For a terrible moment I thought he was going to throw himself on to the pyre, the expression on his face was so desperate. Then I saw something in his hands ... a bundle of fabric.

'Clothing ... ' Tashi said. 'What is he ... ?'

He held the bundle high. I saw the glimmer of a brass button in the firelight and suddenly understood.

'It's his uniform.'

Chen threw the jacket and trousers on to the pyre. A flurry of sparks went up.

He remained motionless for a few long moments, his head bowed as if in prayer. Then he turned away and took his place once more in the crowd.

'He's taking such a risk,' Tashi said. 'All we need to do is alert the police …'

'I think he's beyond caring,' I replied. 'He looks like a broken man.'

Gradually the refugees dispersed. The holy man took his leave. Chen walked across to us and stood there for a while before summoning the power to speak. I felt Tashi tense up beside me.

'There are two ways now … ' Chen said slowly. 'And it is you that must choose. In any case I will not go back to China.'

He hung his head and the world seemed to hush. The only sound was the mysterious creaking and shifting of the ashes as the pyre cooled.

'You can report me for the murder of my son,' Chen continued softly. 'I will accept the consequences. If not, I will take a different path; try to be true to Zhong's life ...'

'How do you mean?' I asked.

'He was ashamed of what I did,' Chen said. 'I want to act now in a way he would be proud of. He wanted to help the people of Tibet. There are many ways I can continue that quest.'

Tashi pulled me away so that we could talk privately.

'You don't think it's a trick?' I said.

'We must do what Zhong would have wanted,' Tashi whispered. 'If there is a chance his father can change, don't you think he would want us to try that? What purpose will it serve for him to spend the rest of his life in prison?'

'But he's getting away with murder.'

'I think he's sincere,' Tashi continued. 'You can see it in his eyes.'

We walked back through the camp with Chen. The sun was just setting, kids kicking up clouds of dust as they played football on an improvised pitch. Women were sitting on a nearby stone wall chatting gently to each other while they waited for the evening prayers.

'How do we know you will really change?' I asked Chen.

'After I shot Zhong,' he replied slowly. 'I walked into the forest. I sat down by a tree and did not move for two days and nights. I was consumed with regret and sorrow.'

We reached Tashi's family tent. We could hear Karma and Tashi's parents talking quietly inside.

'I went to the river,' Chen said. 'Threw myself in. I didn't try to swim, didn't try to float. I just let myself be swept away, wanting the punishment I deserved.'

Footsteps padded up behind us. It was one of the monks, bearing a terracotta pot in his hands.

'Here are the ashes of your friend,' he said respectfully. He presented the urn to Tashi, bowed deeply then turned away.

'I felt myself drowning,' Chen continued. 'It felt right. My entire life has been tainted by bitterness and anger and I knew this was the only way to purge it. Later I came around and found to my surprise that I was still alive. I had been swept on to a sandbank. I took the first breaths of my new life.'

The sun was setting and our eyes turned to the north, seeking out Everest on the skyline. Straight away we found it, the snows of the South-West Face glittering with reflected orange-red sunlight. It felt like an image from a movie. Like it was being projected on a screen. All the pain and wonder and drama of our climb was somehow suspended in that moment as I felt Tashi and Chen come to my side.

'You should take these,' Tashi said to Chen, handing him the urn.

Chen clutched the clay pot, pressing it to his chest. At that precise moment an extraordinary thing happened. A huge bird took off from the branches of the tree above us, wings beating hard against the canopy and showering us in leaves. We stood back, startled, as the creature circled upwards.

'An eagle,' Chen exclaimed.

The bird flew out across the valley, in a dead straight line for Everest. Chen watched it fly for a few seconds.

'I will keep my side of this bargain,' he said earnestly. 'You will see.'

Chen left us. Tashi and I continued staring towards the mountain. The eagle became a dot, seeming to melt into snow as it vanished. With every second the colours shifted and changed, the reds and oranges intensifying as darkness crept closer.

'Will you go back to Everest one day?' Tashi whispered.

I took the shrine bell from my pocket, turning the precious artefact in my hands as I thought about her question. The sacred little bell had now been high on Everest on two occasions but still had not reached the top. I thought about my friend Kami, about his girlfriend Shreeya, and felt a longing to see them, to tell them all about the adventure I had just had. They would be so happy to know I had been on Everest. So happy to know the shrine bell had once again been on the mountain.

'I will,' I told her. 'Unfinished business.'

Tashi took the bell from me, holding it reverently in her hands.

'You've been above eight thousand metres,' she said. 'So you know you can handle the altitude. All you have to do now is find your way on to a proper expedition with some backup and Sherpa support.'

'How about you?' I asked her. 'Want to come with me?'

Tashi turned to me. Her deeply black eyes were dancing with stars. She slipped her hand into mine.

'I'll have a think about that,' she said. 'Maybe I will.'

Karma's voice rang out.

'Hey! You two! It's freezing out there when the sun goes down.'

'Coming!' Tashi called.

We took one last look at Everest, then turned to the welcoming warmth of the tent.

END OF BOOK TWO

WITH THANKS TO ...

I would like to register my thanks to all the Tibetan people who helped during my journey to Everest. The trip across the Friendship Bridge was a magical introduction to the world's highest land, taking me high on to the plateau where I was fortunate to explore Shekar Dzong and Tingri, two of the great historic trading towns of southern Tibet.

Readers keen to read up-to-date and credible reports describing what is happening to the people of Tibet should check out: Human Rights Watch (*www.hrw.org*) and Amnesty International (*www.amnesty.org*). Tibetan-run websites include: Free Tibet (*www.freetibet.org*) and the Tibetan Centre for Human Rights and Democracy (*www.tchrd.org*).

The second book in the 'The Everest Files' series has been an 'interesting' writing experience, not least because it has been scribbled down in trains, planes and automobiles (though not while driving!) over the course of a year and a half in which I have talked in about 150 schools around the UK and overseas.

During that time the Everest Reading Challenge has been running and I want to thank Nicky Hetherington, Katy Fletcher and Amy McKay for their early help and support. Up in Scotland I want to extend a big tartan-flavoured literary hug to Maggie Gray, Yvonne Manning, Mandy Wilson and Duncan Wright.

Heading down further south Matt and Miriam Bartlett have often provided a welcome refuge in London (and scarily incisive literary judgement!). Judy Leden and Chris Dawes have also been wonderfully welcoming in the Peak.

Being out on the road (globally) as a touring author needs plenty of publisher support and in this I am fortunate to have the backup of Jon Barton, John Coefield, Victoria Halliday and Lorna Hargreaves. Thanks team V! Your rapid-response capabilities are second to none. PS Can you get 1,000 copies of *The Everest Files* out to Khartoum for next Tuesday please? I'm doing some schools out there!

Sarah Darby has once again been brilliant, creating inventive new chapter heading illustrations of great charm and quality. I also want to thank the members of my writers' group – Sarah Mussi and Caroline Johnston – for feedback given.

Finally, special thanks to Ruth Eastham who helped the story grow in so many important ways.

ABOUT THE AUTHOR

Matt Dickinson is an award-winning writer and filmmaker with a passion for climbing and adventure. During his filmmaking career he has worked as a director/cameraman for National Geographic television, the Discovery Channel, the BBC and Channel 4. His film projects have taken him to Antarctica, Africa and the Himalaya, often in the company of the world's leading climbers and expeditioners. His most notable film success was *Summit Fever* in which Matt reached the summit of Everest via the treacherous North Face. His book *The Death Zone* tells the true story of that ascent and has become a bestseller in many different countries.

Matt is currently Patron of Reading at Lady Manners School in Bakewell and continues to climb and explore. In January 2013 he summitted Mount Aconcagua, which, at 6,965 metres, is the highest peak in the world outside the Himalaya. Currently, he is planning an ascent of Denali in Alaska, one of the 'Seven Summits'.

Recently Matt has started writing fiction for teenage readers. His debut thriller series *Mortal Chaos* was well-received by critics and readers alike. Matt followed this up with the first of three *The Everest Files* books, which has proven to be very popular. *North Face* is the hotly anticipated second title in the trilogy. When he's not writing, Matt tours the UK, speaking at schools and colleges and inspiring a new generation of adventurers.

Fascinated by Everest?

Want to know more about the world's highest peak?

The Everest Files website is packed full of fascinating facts and features.

- Find out about Everest, the Himalaya and the effect global warming is having on the area. Geographical facts with study guides for teachers.
- Watch the summit footage taken by *The Everest Files* author Matt Dickinson after his epic North Face ascent.
- Discover more about the Sherpa people and their way of life.
- See an interview with Jordan Romero, the 13-year-old boy who became the youngest person ever to summit Everest.
- Learn more about *The Everest Files* trilogy, including a video message from author Matt Dickinson.

If you would like an author visit from Matt Dickinson for your school or club, contact details can be found on the website.

www.everestfiles.com

Follow Ryan Hart's adventure in
The Everest Files books ...

The Everest Files.

A missing teenage climber. A trail of deadly clues.
Mystery on the world's highest peak.

Killer Storm.

A helicopter crash on the Kangshung Face.
A white-out blizzard rolls in. The scene is set for
the ultimate Everest drama.

Find out more about *The Everest Files* at
www.everestfiles.com